Coldarius: The Betrayal
Book II
D.L. Hannah

Contents

Isis. We did this five times, baby! Yeah! We did that!

Chapter 1

Princess Opal was led down a long, candlelit corridor connected to the medical chamber where King Carlomon was waiting. He sat beside Queen Dellah's bedside with his head resting in his hands. Not wanting to awaken the queen, she quietly approached the bed. He didn't notice the soft hand resting on his shoulder.

"Father," she said. "How is she?"

He slowly raised his head up and turned to look at her.

"Princess Opal? You're here." He stood and embraced her. "You're finally here! Thank The One for providing a safe journey."

She hugged her father tightly, peering around him at her lying on the bed. "I was told they needed blood. They can have as much as they need to save her life."

He braced his hands on her shoulders and bowed his head.

"Father? What is it?" She looked closely at her. She was so still. Too still. She fought off a wave of dizziness. "No! Dellah?"

She stepped around him and reached for her sister's hand. It was cool to the touch. Her eyes filled with tears. "By the Heavens, no!" She turned to him. "She can't be gone! Father, I got here as fast as I could!"

"It's not your fault. Dr Krause said a blood clot traveled to her lungs and caused a pulmonary embolism. She was...struggling to breathe before she passed. There was nothing we could do to save her."

She burst into tears. "Oh, Dellah! I'm so sorry!"

Before she left for Earth, the twins had been very close. She cursed herself for not being around when she was needed the most. She buried her head into her sister's shoulder and sobbed. He laid a hand on her hair, supporting her. A large crowd had gathered outside the palace to mourn for their queen.

Although the Coldarians were glad to see Princess Opal had returned, they were saddened it was due to Queen Dellah's passing. The Platirians were still in a state of shock—over the queen's death and learning she'd had a twin sister.

"Did you see her?" asked Moira Thornswaithe. "She looks just like Queen Dellah! One could never tell them apart!"

"Where has she been all this time?" asked Theo Lightengate. "Why didn't she come to Platirius when the queen got married?"

"She's been doing missions for King Carlomon since her teens," said Sergeant Lionus. "She's one of our best spies."

"A spy?! I can't imagine wanting to live among Humans for that long! They're atrocious," said Dora Reese.

"Her work is important," said Sergeant Lionus. "We've acquired a lot of knowledge about the Humans. After all this time, they still think little green Beings are running around the galaxy. It just goes to show how stupid they are! We could attack them at any time and win."

He looked up at the high tower of the medical chamber. "I hope we do. I know what King Carlomon wants, but we won't gain anything by bringing them to Coldarius."

Corporal Chattingway said, "If Earth was absorbed into Coldarius, it would make us more powerful."

Corporal Lox, a Maieman soldier, spat on the ground. "What makes you think King Dubian wouldn't want Earth for Platirius? You joined them, not the other way around."

General Iham gave him a chilling slow perusal. He was a peaceful MaleForm, but the queen's death had set him on edge. "And what would you know of it? You're from Maieman. Your planet is nowhere near as prosperous as Coldarius. Shut your mouth, soldier, or I'll shut it for you."

The young soldier saluted the general. "Excuse me, General Iham. I spoke out of turn, sir!"

"Yeah, you did. Our queen's body isn't cold yet, but you have the audacity to throw stones at us! Make sure you don't make the same mistake twice."

He pointed a finger in his face. "We don't need all of you Maiemans here anyway. If Major Kron dies on Kikhani, I'll personally ship you back to your king. But while you're here, you'll show proper respect for our realm. Do you understand?"

His threat was for all of the Maieman soldiers.

"Yes, General Iham! I didn't mean to show disrespect, sir." His eyes slid to Gallium, who was watching from a distance.

Gallium strolled over to Corporal Lox and stood in front of him. The young soldier fought to keep his face impassive under his icy scrutiny.

Gallium's tone was colder than the sheets of ice clinging to the window panes. "You didn't salute me."

Corporal Lox cried out as his arm involuntarily jerked from his side. It bent and conformed until his hand rested on the side of his skull in a crisp salute.

The icy fire in his sea-green eyes struck fear in the hearts of all the Maieman soldiers. "I control the oxygen in your blood, Lox. I wouldn't insult our home again or you might find yourself drained like a well."

He fought to control his breathing while beads of sweat ran down his trembling face. "Forgive me, General Barrios!"

Gallium backed away and looked around at the crowd. "The B-shift is to stand guard over the queen. A-shift, return to the military chamber and prepare to relieve them at dawn. The rest of you should go home. There's nothing more we can do for Queen Dellah. She's with her family now. King Dubian..." his voice trailed off, "is of no use to us at the moment."

"She's with a WomanForm that looks just like her!" said Sandi Childler. She pointed to a royal craft. "She just arrived in that craft."

Princess Opal, thought Gallium. "I'm not surprised her sister came to be with her. Coldarius's royal family is very small. Go on home now. We'll keep you informed of what's going on."

At his order, the crowd dispersed with a few melancholy glances back at the palace. The Coldarians and the Platirians had suffered a great loss. No one knew how or if they'd recover from it.

Dr. Krause opened the medical chamber's door. "General Barrios? Princess Opal has asked to see you."

He sighed and nodded. "I'm coming."

Turning to General Iham, he said, "Are you going to be alright? This is all new to me, but I'll do whatever you need me to do."

The old general rocked his head back and forth. "I've known her since she was an InfantForm. She died so young! What on Coldarius will we do without her now? That moron doesn't have what it takes to lead an army of ants. He'll destroy everything she's built in half a year's span."

Gallium placed a hand on his shoulder. "We won't let her legacy be tainted by his incompetence. She's worked too hard to build both kingdoms into what they are."

General Iham nodded. "You should get going and see what the princess wants. I'm sure she and the king will want to bring her back to Coldarius for the DeathCeremony. I can't wait to see what King Dubian says when he hears that."

"If he tries to stop her family from giving her a proper burial, he'll have me to answer to. The only reason he's bringing the Maieman soldiers here is to outnumber us Coldarians, but his plans will fail. I promised Queen Dellah I'd protect what she's built and I will."

"I know you will, son." He wiped a hand over his eyes. "She was a good friend to us, wasn't she?"

Gallium looked up at the window of the chamber where she lay resting. "She was the best, General Iham. The very best of us."

Princess Opal was holding Princess Revari to her bosom when he arrived.

"Well, aren't you just lovely? You're the most perfect baby I've ever seen," she murmured. She looked up at King Carlomon. "Father, surely we're not going to let her idiot husband raise the princesses on his own, are we? From what you've told me, he's in no state of mind to provide proper parenting."

"I plan to take Dellah and her daughters back to Coldarius with me. I'll have her buried in the family plot and raise her ChildForms in our kingdom." He looked around the state-of-the-art medical chamber. "We've merged with Platirius, but now that she's gone, what good is any of it?"

"If you break the merger, won't the economies suffer?"

He nodded. "Yes, but we'll manage. We weren't destitute before the merger, and we never will be. I don't want to watch that fool dismantle everything she's accomplished."

She looked down at Princess Revari. "Maybe we won't have to," she said.

He removed Queen Dellah's wedding ring and tossed it into the fireplace. "What do you mean?"

"Now that I've learned what Gallium can do, I think it would be best if we used him as a weapon. If he slays King Dubian, Platirius will be absorbed into Coldarius. We'd have all the wealth and power Dellah acquired for the princesses to inherit without having to deal with him. With Gallium, we could easily remove him from the equation."

A familiar feeling of dread washed over him. "Are you suggesting we murder him for power?"

She crossed her legs and adjusted the baby in her arms. "Why not? He'd do it to us in a blink of a star."

He pointed to Princess Revari. "He's still their father. What would we tell them once they reach adult stages—that we killed their father to protect their financial interests?"

She laid her across her shoulder. "We wouldn't have to tell them anything. Princess Vivant is older. She'd still remember him, but barely."

He handed her a bottle. "She took a few ounces while Dellah was..." His voice broke.

"Sit down and rest a bit. I'm here now. We'll get through this together as a family."

She waited until he was seated before she continued. "As for this one," she said, placing the nipple in the baby's mouth, "she'll have no memories of him. I think it'll be best if we get rid of the last of King Anemi's cursed family. We shouldn't allow their dementedness to affect the princesses."

"It's still murder. I can't go along with that."

She sighed impatiently. "Even if it's what's best for everyone? What if he decides to take us out? With all the soldiers he's bringing in from Maieman, he could easily do it."

"You're forgetting one thing," he told her.

Her silver eyes scanned his face. "What's that?"

He looked over her shoulder. "We have Gallium."

"You wanted to see me, Princess Opal?"

She pivoted to the sound of his deep voice. He was so handsome, he took her breath away. "Yes, I did. Hello, Gallium. I'm so sorry we had to see each other under these circumstances."

He bowed to her. "It's nice to see you again too."

Gently, he stroked a finger across the tiny princess's hand. At his touch, she raised it in the air but didn't awaken.

Princess Opal smiled at her. "I thought Princess Vivant was a gorgeous baby, but she is absolutely breathtaking."

His eyes roamed over the sleeping baby. "Yes, she is. She looks just like her mother."

"And her aunt," she said. "She'll be a beautiful WomanForm once she grows up. Not that I'm vain or anything." She cast a sober glance at Queen Dellah. "Why in the galaxy did this happen, Gallium? Why would The One take my sister when he knew how much we all needed her?"

"I know it's hard, but we don't sit high enough to question His will. He wanted her for reasons only He knows. I wish it weren't true, but it is."

He turned to King Carlomon. "Your Highness, General Iham and I have made arrangements for you and Princess Opal to rest in the palace. Don't worry. Your chambers will be on the opposite wing—as far away from King Dubian as possible. Queen Dellah had Princess Revari's nursery chamber constructed weeks ago, and the NurseForms can take care of her while you rest."

She kissed the baby's hand. "No. My niece will sleep with me in my chamber. I understand what NurseForms are for, but we've never used them on Coldarius. That's why our familial ties are stronger than the Platirians. They've relied on them while we care for our families ourselves. She just lost her mother. I won't have her around strangers."

Princess Opal adjusted the expensive blanket around her. "That will confuse you, won't it, Baby?" she cooed. "Aunt Opal is here now. I'm going to take good care of you and your sister, all right?"

He bowed his head. "Whatever you feel is best."

Her chilly gaze was reminiscent of Queen Dellah. "You and I are going to whip these Platirians into shape. Had I known of the difficulties she suffered while carrying Princess Revari, I would've been here to help. I won't fail my sister again."

King Carlomon folded Queen Dellah's arms on top of her chest. "Let's get her moved into the worship chamber and have the burial staff prepare her to be taken to Coldarius. Then we'll turn in for the night. I'm eager to leave here as soon as possible. It's far too ominous for my tastes."

"I'll take care of the arrangements, My King. The cleaning staff will show you and Princess Opal where you'll sleep, and I'll have Princess Revari's bed brought to your chambers."

Her quick peck on the cheek startled him. "Thank you, Gallium. I feel much better knowing you're here to run things."

"You're welcome. I'm here for whatever you need."

She paused. "What will we do about King Dubian?"

Titillated by the dark look that came into his eyes, she shuddered. "We'll deal with him in time. Right now, let's get you comfortable."

General Iham read the note on his palm and ran to find Gallium. He was almost out of breath by the time he reached him. "It's over! King Hitam just conceded. Platirius has defeated Kikhani!"

He let out a slow whistle. "So the kid really did it, huh? He ended the war."

Major Kron was only a few years younger than Gallium, but he was an outsider to Coldarians and Platirians. His extreme cockiness and self-centered ways didn't help his plight. It didn't matter if he'd defeated one of the most powerful kings in the galaxy—he'd never be accepted among them.

General Iham nodded. "Yes. I suppose King Dubian will be eager to appoint him to general now."

"If he does, he'll never outrank you or I by merit. Any achievement he gets will be gifted to him by the king."

General Iham sucked his teeth. "That's what I've always hated about Beings like King Dubian. He never earned anything and was given everything."

"I heard he stole it all. Dimaro was supposed to be king, but he made sure that didn't happen."

"Well, yes, that's true. No one knows how he did it, but I believe he ended him. The body was never found."

General Iham frowned. "He'll never know how it feels to claim something you've worked for with blood and sweat." Looking up into Space, he said, "The galaxy is going to hell, Gallium. It's all going to hell and there's nothing we can do about it."

Gallium placed a hand on the older general's shoulder. "Hey, when did you start getting so pessimistic? Our queen worked hard to build all that we have now. We can't let her down by letting the Platirians piss on it."

General Iham disconnected the transmission on his palm. "You're right about that. I'll follow her to the grave before I allow that imbecile to sink us. What he does with Platirius is his business, but as for Coldarius, I'm not surprised King Carlomon has come to bring us home."

"I wish I had thought of that before my daughter died."

"King Carlomon! Please accept my deepest condolences on your loss."

They shook hands. "Thank you. I've lost my wife and now one of my daughters." He looked up at the window of King Dubian's bed chamber. To the generals' surprise, he spit violently on the ground.

He'd always carried himself with dignity, but the loss of his daughter coupled with her husband's theatrics had awakened deeply rooted seeds of contempt. "I won't let any more Coldarians die because of him. We're leaving Platirius."

Corporal Canob ran up to them and bowed. "King Carlomon, General Iham, and General Barrios, the food crafts are circling around the dining chamber. They can't get in because King Dubian ordered us to close the borders!"

Gallium swore. "I guess he expects his subjects to starve."

Corporal Canob grimaced. "The dining staff don't know what to do. Operations have been shut down until the food crafts can land."

"Re-open the borders," ordered King Carlomon. "I don't rule Platirius, but I won't let them starve."

Corporal Canob saluted him and hurried to carry out his order.

"He's out of his mind. He should be de-throned," said King Carlomon.

"He'd have to be murdered for that to happen. He has no family left to assume the throne until the princesses grow up," said Princess Opal. "Or he'd need to remarry again for another queen to rule. Dellah was the diplomat. I have no interest in running Platirius."

Gallium blinked. *Is it possible?* "You've never met him, have you?"

She shook her head. "No, nor do I want to. I agree with my father. We should leave right now. The atmosphere seems dark and evil without Dellah. I won't have the princesses raised here."

"I wonder how he'd react if he saw you," said General Iham.

"I think we're about to find out," said Gallium.

King Dubian appeared at the palace's gate. "Why are those crafts landing? I gave specific orders to close my borders."

"How do you think your Beings will eat? Do you expect them to run out to the gardens and start boiling flowers?"

The ugliness he'd hid in his heart was now etched on his face for all to witness. "They can rot for all I care! Everything will remain just as Dellah wants it to be."

"Are you aware Beings actually ate when my daughter was alive? She never closed the borders!" shouted King Carlomon. "This is why we lost her! She had to do everything around here because of your incompetence! You should've had her resting at the first sign of trouble with the pregnancy!"

"But there were no complications. She just had a healthy delivery with Princess Vivant! They're both fine!"

Everyone stared at him. A frenzied look was in his eyes.

His mind is unraveling right in front of us, thought General Iham.

"General Iham."

"Yes, My King?"

"It's time to go. I've had enough of this."

"Yes, King Carlomon!"

King Dubian watched him hurry away. "You're just going to leave without seeing Dellah and Princess Vivant? What kind of father abandons his daughter after she gives birth?"

King Carlomon grabbed him by his collar, ripping his costly shirt. "You have some nerve asking me that when you were too weak to hold your own daughter! Had I known you were this crazy, I never would've allowed you to marry my Dellah!" Towering over him by several inches, he nearly lifted him from the ground. "If you think you're going to ruin my granddaughters, you're gravely mistaken!"

He looked at him and Gallium as if they were the ones who had gone mad. "I haven't ruined anyone. Dellah is the strongest WomanForm I know. No one has the power to destroy her. What's wrong with you?"

King Carlomon shook him until his teeth rattled. "No! What's wrong with *you,* you *foolish creature?*" he roared.

Princess Opal stepped out of the shadows and grabbed his arm. "Father! Please don't! He's not worth arguing with," she cried.

King Dubian slowly turned to face her. A strange light dawned in his eyes. "My Queen, you shouldn't be up so soon—you've just given birth to our daughter. Please tell your father I've not allowed you to come to harm. Haven't I always protected you?"

She took a step back as he advanced toward her. "What's this? You've never been afraid of me. What have they been telling you to turn you against me?"

Her eyes filled with tears. "I'm not Dellah! I'm her sister."

His eyes fixed on her, blinking rapidly. "If you're trying to drive me insane, you're succeeding, my love." He moved closer to her. "Come, let me take you back to the medical chamber so you can rest."

King Carlomon lifted his BrainStaff. "If you take one more step near her, I'll cut you down."

He stopped in his tracks and looked at him.

"She isn't Dellah. Queen Elia and I had twin daughters."

He whipped his head around at her, his eyes widening in shock. "I've never seen the fear in my wife's eyes that I see in yours," he murmured. "It has to be true. A twin sister! Why has no one informed me of this until now?" he demanded.

"It wasn't your business to know," King Carlomon stated coldly.

General Iham rejoined them. "We're ready, King Carlomon."

"Ready for what?"

King Carlomon shifted his BrainStaff to the opposite side. "Ready to leave this hellhole you call home, Dubian. I'm taking my daughters, my granddaughters, and all of my subjects home. We're finished here. Today. Forever."

"I've alerted the staff in our worship chamber. Everything will be prepared for Queen Dellah's DeathCeremony."

"You sound foolish, General Iham! There isn't going to be a DeathCeremony for Dellah. She isn't *dead*!"

King Carlomon had grown weary of him. "General Barrios, please have the soldiers escort King Dubian to the Chamber of Despair. He's not fit to rule Platirius at this time."

"What? I'm not going anywhere, and if any dirty Coldarians touch me, I'll have them killed!"

"With what soldiers?" asked Gallium. "Look around you. Most of the soldiers here are Coldarians. Do you know how easy it would be to cut off your head and take this planet?"

He tightened his grip on his arm. "All King Carlomon has to do is order it and I'll gladly spill your blood into the streets. But he doesn't want Platirius. He wants to go home. We all do, and that's what we're going to do."

He nodded to the soldiers. "Let's make sure he's locked down well."

King Dubian shouted when the soldiers seized his arms. "Take your filthy hands off me!"

"Filthy?" echoed King Carlomon. "It was my daughter who draped silk across your pathetic behind. You looked and dressed like a pauper before she upgraded you. You weren't even articulate enough to properly address other royals until she trained you like a monkey."

He pointed at him. "You were nothing before she came into your life, and you're nothing now. You won't deny her the honor of having a DeathCeremony."

"What are you doing?" cried Princess Vivant. "Release my father! Immediately!"

Everyone turned to see her running down the palace stairs. King Carlomon stretched out his arms and picked her up.

"What on Platirius is happening, Grandfather?" She tried to struggle out of his firm grasp. "Where are they taking my father?"

"Look at me, Princess Vivant," said King Carlomon. "Your father isn't mentally sound. He needs time to rest in the Chamber of Despair. The mental wellness staff will take good care of him until he's well again. You want him to get better, don't you?"

She sobbed. "But I don't understand. Why is he sick? And where is Mother? Mother will take care of him. She takes care of all of us."

Princess Opal stifled a sob watching him hold her. "I'm taking you, your mother, and baby sister back to Coldarius. We'll sit down and discuss everything once we're home, okay?" He reared back to look into her lovely face. "Is that all right? Do you trust your Grandfather?"

She enveloped him in a fierce hug. "Of course I do. You're the wisest king I know."

Gallium smirked at King Dubian.

Peering over his shoulder, she said, "Hello, Aunt Opal. Will you be staying with us for a while?"

She sniffed and grabbed her hand. Holding it to her face, she said, "I'll be around for as long as you need me, darling."

She beamed. "Mother will be so happy to hear that!"

The adults buried their sadness in front of her. None of them could bear to break her heart. King Carlomon nodded to Gallium.

"Let's go, King Dubian. If you don't want to scare your daughter any more than she already is, I suggest you go quietly."

He gave him a lofty grin. "Who are you to give me orders? You're a freak. A mistake of Satan himself! Your MotherForm should've ended you while you were in her womb!"

Gallium closed the distance between them. "If you don't shut your mouth right now, you're going to wish yours had closed her thighs on your head. I may be a freak, but I wasn't born in sin like you. You're the product of a whore getting pregnant by a married MaleForm. You have zero room to throw stones."

He trembled when a vein in Gallium's neck writhed under his skin. "What are you? What does Dellah see in you?"

Gallium's harsh laugh rang out. "That's what Coldarians have been asking since we learned she would marry you. Maybe if you hadn't murdered your brother, we wouldn't be here right now, but here we are."

He leaned down to whisper in his ear. "And trust me, it'll be much easier for me to kill you than it was for you to get rid of him. I heard he wounded you badly before you ended him. As for me, you're not worth putting the sweat on my brow."

He looked frantically around at the grinning soldiers. "I never should've allowed you Coldarians to come here. I'll ask Dellah to send you all back!"

Gallium chuckled. "Let's get him out of here. We have a long journey ahead of us."

By the time King Dubian was locked away inside the Chamber of Despair, all the Coldarians were standing outside the palace's gates with King Carlomon, Princess Opal, and the princesses.

Dora Reese wrung her hands. "Thank you for opening the borders so we could unload the food, General Barrios. But what on Platirius will we do? Who will lead us now?"

His eyes scanned the group of frightened Platirians—most of them who had grown to love and accept Queen Dellah. They were mourning her loss too. He looked up at King Carlomon sitting on his horse with Princess Vivant.

The king looked at the extravagantly decorated chambers nestled around the enormous palace and sighed. "Platirius is dying. It may have defeated Kikhani, but without a decent ruler, your enemies will pluck your king like a flea on a dog."

Tears filled Sandi Childler's eyes. She and Dora held hands and listened.

"Platirius is in no position to go to war with another planet, nor is your king worth dying for. I'm willing to take some of you to Coldarius, but I can't move everyone. My kingdom is a lot smaller than this one. It would be best to look to other territories to make a new home. I don't believe Platirius will last another year."

Dora Reese dried her eyes. "I want to go where the princesses are. They're the last of Queen Dellah," she said. "If you'll let us, we want to make the journey with you, King Carlomon."

Most of the WomenForms were ready to follow the Coldarians, but a few, along with the Platirian-born MaleForms and the Maieman soldiers, stayed behind on Platirius.

Sergeant Fontine had been born and raised on Platirius. A long-time loyalist to King Anemi, he was overjoyed to see the Coldarians leave. Not believing WomenForms should have authority over MaleForms, he hadn't liked watching Queen Dellah assume control of Platirius.

His narrow gaze held barely veiled contempt for Coldarius's king. "Much respect to you, King Carlomon, but we need to stay behind and pick up the pieces. King Dubian won't be in the position he's in forever."

The sound of his nasally voice irritated Gallium. King Carlomon raised his chin. "Should I take that as a threat, Sergeant?"

An evil glint sparkled in his eyes. "Oh no, Your Majesty. I mean no ill will toward you. It's just the Amorous family has always ran Platirius for generations. It may not have been King Dubian's right to rule, but what's done is done. As the last surviving member, he has a duty to uphold his father's legacy."

He combed his unruly beard with his fingers. "He can easily find another WomanForm—maybe someone not as feisty and headstrong as Queen Dellah was—and start over again."

This time, the Coldarians didn't miss the edge in his voice. He laughed and raised his hands when Gallium and the rest of the Coldarian soldiers advanced toward him. "Hey! I had nothing against her! I just think our king got a bit lazy following her around like a little puppy is all."

His beady eyes fell on Princess Opal holding Princess Revari in her arms. "If he marries an addle-brained WomanForm to give him sons, then he won't need to worry about one of your granddaughters taking the throne."

"My granddaughters are no longer his concern. Or yours. You seem to have a lot to say about my daughter now that she's no longer with us. I doubt you would've said any of it to her face. But since she isn't here to defend herself, allow me to ease your anxiety."

The blast from his BrainStaff severed Sergeant Fontine's skull in half. His brain slid out and dropped to the floor with a hard *thuck*. He fell face-first into the road, surrounded by screams and cries of disgust mixed in with laughter as dark red blood pooled around his body.

King Carlomon's spit landed squarely on the dead MaleForm. "I'm advising every Platirian to be mindful of what you say about us. If you despise Coldarians so intensely, you should thank The One you no longer have to interact with us. Those of you who'd like to stay behind with your king, please be my guest."

He slapped the reins against his horse. "Let us go."

Only a small group was left to stand around the fallen soldier. Princess Vivant stared at Sergeant Fontine's body and smiled. Princess Revari cooed as her grandfather's horse rounded a curve and carried them out of Platirius.

Chapter 2

Princess Vivant hadn't stopped crying since learning she'd never see her mother again. She stood on a balcony in King Carlomon's palace for hours, refusing to allow him or Princess Opal to comfort her.

"What should we do?" asked Princess Opal. "She's been up there on her own for quite some time. I've just received a transmission from the Chief Minister. They're waiting for your order to begin Dellah's DeathCeremony."

He rubbed his hands in his hair. "I honestly don't know what we can do. She was very close to her mother. I don't regret bringing them here to live with me. The One only knows what would happen had they been left to fend for themselves with their worthless father."

She patted his shoulder. "You acted in their best interest, Father. If he's wise, he'll stay on Platirius once he's released."

"Yes, but who will release him? There are no rulers left on Platirius to oversee its affairs. I say we allow it to be conquered and be done with it."

"But if another territory takes it, they'll inherit enormous power. King Anemi conquered many realms in his lifespan. Any enemies of his are our enemies too. If anyone should absorb Platirius, it should be us."

He leaned over the windowsill to check on Princess Vivant. "Let's keep our voices low. I don't want her to hear us."

He sat on the far side of the study so they'd be out of her earshot. "And inherit all the evil that comes with it? Platirius was built on millions of years of theft, forced copulation, and murder by the Amorous family."

He shuddered. "It wouldn't just be the power we'd inherit, it would be the ghosts of all the poor souls that got caught up in their thirst for domination. Dellah was strong enough to handle it, but I pity any WomanForm wanting to step in to fill her shoes."

She righted a painting on the wall. "I met her husband briefly and that was enough. I don't know how she managed to deal with him for all these years. He's completely unhinged. Clearly, her death has sent him spiraling out of control. He refuses to admit she *is* dead. That alone renders him unfit to rule."

She crossed her arms over her chest and began to pace. "Coldarius is made of pure energy. We have none of Platirius's curses."

He raised a brow and observed her.

Has she erased the past from her memory?

"Maybe our energy cancelled out Platirius's negative energy. It thrived as long as Dellah was alive. Surely there's a reason for that. Ah! The PotterBerry wine has arrived. I think I need a glass. Would you like some?"

He rubbed his tired eyes. "I could use some."

She poured two glasses of the fragrant wine made of plums and sweet PotterBerries and handed one to him. Its cool, refreshing taste lifted her mood a bit. She nursed the glass, mulling over her thoughts.

"Father, it's the only way. Platirius is a mess right now. We can't leave it in his hands. Did you hear that old soldier? He was practically singing about how happy he was to see Dellah gone. I suspect many of the Platirian MaleForms share his sentiments."

He drained his glass and reached for the flask. "If they use their witless mouths to disrespect my daughter's memory like he did, they'll be sharing a burial plot with him."

"And there lies the rub. They're ignorant and antiquated. The Platirian WomenForms will never advance as long as misogyny and tyranny exist." She touched his hand. "We can do it. We can keep Platirius from crumbling and preserve it for the princesses. Either of them would make a far better leader than the Amorous MaleForms."

He gently squeezed her hand. "You and Dellah have always been progressive thinkers. I think it's a wonderful idea, but there's never been a WomanForm ruler in any realm. If Princess Vivant or Princess Revari ascended to the throne, they'd be the first to accomplish such a feat."

Her eyes lit up with enthusiasm. "Change will come. It must. Princess Revari is still an InfantForm, but do you see how observant she is? Those sparkling eyes don't miss anything and her reflexes are strong for such a young Being. She won't allow anyone to hold her without a fuss except you, Princess Vivant, Gallium, or I."

He smiled. "Yes, she has her mother's fighting spirit."

"As for Princess Vivant, she's a born leader. She has the confidence and carriage Dellah had. I say Platirius would thrive in either of their hands, just as it did when she was in charge."

"What has you so charged up about WomenForms ruling planets? You've always been a champion for equal rights, but since you've returned, you've been adamant concerning what's to be done with Platirius. Did something happen on Earth you haven't told me about?"

She rolled her eyes. "Human women still aren't allowed to vote. I remember a mission I completed as far back as 1690. It was sickening to watch how some of the Human males treated them. They hanged and burned the women to death on the preposterous notion they were witches and spread outlandish lies for some of the pettiest reasons I'd ever heard."

She threw up her hands. "I know you gave orders not to intervene, and I didn't. But, oh, how I wanted to! I can't imagine Princess Vivant and Princess Revari living under such oppression. Whether we like it or not, Platirius is half of their birthright. One of them should lead it if they wish to."

He set down his glass. "I'm against killing King Dubian for the throne. It goes against every honorable code I believe in."

"You won't have to kill him. Gallium can do it for us. He took out an entire army of Kikhanian soldiers. What's more, he hates King Dubian. I don't think he'll lose any sleep over ending his life. Without another heir of the proper age to take the throne, Gallium could rule until the princesses grow up."

He set the glass down and looked at her.

She raised an eyebrow. "What?"

"So there it is."

She cocked her head to the side. "There what is?"

"You want Gallium to be the king with you at his side."

She refused to meet his eyes. "I never said anything about me."

He smiled at her sadly. "You didn't have to. You're my daughter. I've known you since the day you were born. Do you think I can't see that you're in love with Gallium? You say it won't prick his conscience to kill him, but are you certain of that? You haven't seen him in years. Can you honestly say you know how his mind works?"

She refused to meet his sharp gaze. "Let's say he decides to go along with your plan to get rid of King Dubian. Who do you think will be his queen?"

She started to pour another glass of the PotterBerry wine and spilled it.

Watching her blot it up with a linen napkin, he said, "He's already betrothed to Legend Guilde. He asked her to marry him on the first day of JehovRi. He only went to Platirius because Dellah asked him to. If she hadn't, he would've been happy to remain on Coldarius. Do you really think he'll throw away his entire future to rule another realm?"

Her eyes took on a hard look. "Legend Guilde isn't his 'entire future.' I heard she wants to be a soldier. How on

Coldarius would that work? I doubt he wants to be married to a WomanForm who only thinks of her own ambitions."

"But he does want to marry her, Opal. He's very headstrong and family-oriented. I don't think you'll change his mind any time soon about the WomanForm he loves."

She began to pace in front of him. "How are you so sure he loves her?"

"Please be rational. You've been on Earth for many years. You were well acquainted as ChildForms, but you're a stranger to him now. He wiped out the Kikhanian soldiers under Dellah's order—out of duty. Fighting in a war isn't the same as plotting the murder of a king for personal gain."

He swirled the wine in his glass. "He has a sharp tongue, but he doesn't have an evil bone in his body. He's grown to be a decent and honest MaleForm and deserves to have a life with whom he's chosen. That's Legend Guilde."

She sat in one of the plush chairs, staring at the carved lions mounted on the fireplace. "You sound as if you think highly of her too. She must be very charming to have all the MaleForms on Coldarius under her spell," she said bitterly.

"Daughter, you have no reason to dislike her. The Guildes are good Beings. Her father was killed in a war after I inherited the throne. They've always been loyal to us."

She sat thinking. "Gallium said he made promises to Dellah. He told me she trusted him to ensure the princesses would have a prosperous future."

He stretched out his leg. "And you intend to use their bond to manipulate him into marrying you and taking over Platirius? Dellah asked him to go with her to Platirius, but she never forced him to. It was his choice. You're looking to use his loyalty to her as a stepping stone for your own advancement. Do you think that's fair?"

She sighed in exasperation. "You make it sound as if I'm as devious as Lady Alarah. I won't force him to do anything he doesn't wish to do. I'll simply remind him of the duty he has to my nieces."

"He doesn't need to be reminded. He's aware of his promise to her, but he's under no obligation to do anything for her ChildForms. We are their family. None of it means he has to murder King Dubian and take the throne. He can help you care for the princesses—with Legend at his side."

She jumped out of the chair. "That WomanForm isn't going to raise my nieces!"

He held up a hand as if to hold down her temper. "I never said she would rear them, did I?"

"She isn't royalty—"

"Neither is Gallium. You don't need to belong to a royal family to demonstrate love. We both know he loves Princess Vivant and Princess Revari. How could he not? They're a part of Dellah. But we have no right to fashion that love into a weapon and stick it in his back."

He sat back in the chair and looked at his BrainStaff sitting in a crystal display case. "He's not a tool to be used. He's a Being with goals, dreams, and desires. I understand you want to secure the princesses' future, but we don't need to alter his life to do it."

Angry tears smarted in her eyes.

"I don't want to upset you," said King Carlomon. "None of us expected this, so let's come together and do our best as a family. Scheming and manipulation are signature for Platirians, not Coldarians."

He took her hand in his. "You'll find the MaleForm who's right for you. One who will love you and understand your needs and wants."

She snatched her hand away. "I don't want the 'right' MaleForm. I want Gallium! And if you don't want to help me, I guess I'll have to make things happen for myself."

"Princess Opal!" he cried.

She looked at him with an eerie emptiness he'd witnessed before. "You and Mother had a perfect life. You loved each other and cared about making each other happy. I want that too. I don't want to live as Dellah did—married to an ugly monster who needed a WomanForm to tell him how to think and act!"

His heart sank as he realized the time she'd spent on Earth hadn't changed her. He had hoped—

"Gallium is kind, brave, handsome, and strong. He'll make a wonderful king. How can you not see it? Or maybe you refuse to." She turned away from his outstretched hand. "I'm going to get the princesses ready for the DeathCeremony."

"We have time before it begins. We should talk more about this."

"There's nothing more to say. Apparently, you're thinking of the needs of Legend Guilde over your own daughter's. As long as she lives, she'll never do more for Coldarius than I have. I'm finished with this conversation."

He watched her leave through blurred vision. She was wrong. He wasn't favoring Legend over her—she was the only daughter he had left. When would she understand forcing a MaleForm to love her would never work?

He sighed. She and Dellah had always been so different. She still believed she could force love and acceptance. If he needed to step in to protect Gallium, he would. Even if it meant protecting him from his own daughter.

T he mourners lined up outside the worship chamber to say their goodbyes to the fallen Queen of Platirius. Hundreds of blue and diamond roses covered the crystal DeathCraft that held her body. On her head was a high crown of diamonds that glistened under the soft lights.

She wore a full-length, royal blue gown encrusted in sapphires. Heavy jewelry adorned her neck, wrists, and fingers. Princess Opal had done her makeup in soft shades of blue and silver. Her lips, painted with sleek, shimmery oil, looked smooth and supple.

She was the picture of perfection. It was hard to imagine Death had come to claim her. She looked as if she were asleep.

Princess Vivant sobbed and held onto King Carlomon as Beings stood before the chamber and shared fond memories of her mother. Everyone gave their condolences and admired how beautiful she and Princess Revari were. No one mentioned King Dubian.

Even the Platirians who had journeyed to Coldarius didn't regret leaving Platirius behind. Although the weather was colder than what they were accustomed to, the hearts of the Coldarians were warm and welcoming. Thus, returning to Platirius was the least of their concerns. Many enjoyed the peaceful atmosphere and hoped to gain Coldarian citizenship.

Making a pulchritudinous picture, an impeccably dressed Gallium entered the worship chamber with Legend on his arm. All heads turned to him as he strode toward the royal family and bowed before turning to Queen Dellah to pay his respects. The spectators couldn't help staring at him. He was a good-looking MaleForm.

He lightly touched her hand with his fingertip, struggling to hold back tears. He'd never imagined he'd say goodbye to his dear friend. Legend bowed gracefully, squeezing his hand for support.

"She looks absolutely breathtaking, doesn't she?" she whispered.

He nodded. "She always did. I hope she's happy in The One's realm. We talked about her fears of leaving the princesses, but

I don't think anyone thought it would happen." He looked at Legend. "It's not fair. I know we shouldn't question His will, but I've tried to wrap my mind around why He took her from us and came up empty. She was the glue that held us all together."

Turning his gaze back to the DeathCraft, he said, "Without her, everything fell apart."

She brushed a few strands of his black, curly hair off his face. "I try telling myself He had a bigger assignment only she could accomplish. Coldarius is our world, but we don't belong here. One day, we'll all be called back to our true home. All we can do is take comfort in knowing we'll live in eternal in peace with Him."

"That makes sense, but my heart is still broken and I'm not sure how to mend it. She treated me like an equal—not an outcast." He exhaled. "There'll never be another like her."

She laid her head on his shoulder. "That much is true. She was indeed one of a kind. I'll miss her beautiful face."

"Well, that's odd to hear," said Princess Opal. "Especially since I'm wearing it."

Gallium and Legend turned to face her. Legend gasped.

Princess Opal stared her down. "Oh, that's right. You didn't know Dellah and I were twins. You were attending school on another planet when I left for Earth. My father must've been paying yours quite handsomely to afford the instruction fees."

Still shellshocked, Legend shook her head abruptly. "You— Forgive me for staring, but it's uncanny how much you and Queen Dellah look alike."

Princess Opal smiled ruefully. "Yes, that's why we're called mirror images, Ms. Guilde."

Legend thought she detected a hint of coldness in her tone, but assumed she was angry over losing her sister. However, when she addressed Gallium, her voice heated up faster than a log thrown on a fire.

"I'm so happy you came, Gallium. I couldn't imagine sending her off without her dearest friend here for support."

"I don't want to be here, but I wouldn't have missed saying goodbye to her for anything. I wish we were gathered under happier circumstances." He surveyed the clusters of sad faces in the crowd. "Our lives won't be the same without her."

She rubbed her hand up and down his arm. "You're right. I'm not sure how Father and I will manage with two small ChildForms running around the palace. Princess Vivant is heartbroken and Princess Revari—" she paused to tilt her head closer to him "—doesn't sleep well at night. She only had a few moments to bond with Dellah, but I can tell she misses her."

Legend carefully observed Princess Opal. She had a sinking feeling she didn't like her, but told herself she was being silly. Since they'd just met and didn't know each other well, she had no reason to hold any ill will toward her. Besides, she had just lost her sister. One could hardly expect her to be overly gracious at such a difficult time.

Still, she felt something was off about the way she interacted with Gallium. She'd become accustomed to him receiving a lot of attention from WomenForms. She told herself it was the price of being engaged to an exceptionally attractive MaleForm.

She suspected quite a few WomenForms wanted to be in her shoes. But Princess Opal? She could have any MaleForm she wanted. Well, except hers, of course. Now wasn't the time to embrace insecurity.

He peered into Princess Revari's face. "You're looking more precious every day, little princess." He gently caught the tiny, outstretched hand. "Oh, you want to come to me? Come on then."

When he lifted her from Princess Opal's arms, Legend could've sworn she saw heat reflected in her eyes. She looked uncomfortably away and caught the gaze of Lady Alarah, observing Gallium holding Princess Revari before training her eyes on Legend.

Picking up on her conflicting emotions, she smirked. Legend didn't miss her silent message.

You're no match for her, Legend. Stick to selling flowers.

She turned away from her mocking gaze, forcing herself to concentrate on the baby who was now cooing at Gallium.

"Why am I not surprised you can charm any female in the galaxy?"

He kissed her soft cheek before smiling at Legend. "She's charming me. She'll be quite the heartbreaker when she grows up."

"And you'll be there to keep the MaleForms on notice," declared Princess Opal.

"That's right," he said. "No one gets close to her without me knowing everything about him. Isn't that right?"

Princess Revari continued to babble and grabbed his nose. He and Legend laughed. "She loves my nose for some reason."

He handed her to Princess Opal.

"You're coming to our dining chamber for the Death Celebration feast, right?" she asked.

"Of course." He looked at Legend and squeezed her hand. "We'll be there. Queen Dellah meant a lot to all of us. We owe it to her to give her a good send-off."

He looked around the worship chamber again. "I made sure her space in the royal burial grounds looked the way she would've wanted. I filled it with lots of roses and other nice things."

Princess Opal touched his shoulder. "I'm sure it looks amazing. Thank you for being such a good friend to my sister and my entire family. We've always loved you."

Legend was trying not to overreact, but something about Princess Opal rubbed her the wrong way. She addressed Gallium as if she wasn't standing next to him. Legend knew next to nothing about her, but she was very different from Queen Dellah, who had been the epitome of confidence.

Princess Opal seemed insecure and territorial. But why? If she had been on Earth, then how did she know Gallium well enough to carry on so intimately with him in front of everyone? None of it made sense. Feeling his thumb slide across her wrist made her feel better.

"I loved her too," he told Princess Opal. "I wanted to see her at my wedding. I still can't believe she's gone."

King Carlomon joined them. "She'll be there in spirit, son. I remember how happy she was planning to design your wedding gown, Legend."

Princess Opal stiffened.

"Her seamstress sent over the sketches this morning and I gave the order for her to begin working on it. She's a lovely Being—Marcia Blight. She's here with us from Platirius. In fact, most of the Platirian WomenForms returned with us."

"Thank you, King Carlomon. It was so generous of her to have my gown made." She saw a new group of Beings entering the worship chamber. "No wonder it's so packed. We've never had this many mourners at a DeathCeremony."

"Yes, and they're welcome to stay. There's nothing left on Platirius now. It's a good thing you didn't join King Dubian's army. We'll need you for ours, if you're still interested."

"Oh yes, I am! Thank you so much for the opportunity."

Princess Opal pointedly looked away from Legend, who was beginning to get uncomfortable with her passive-aggressive behavior.

Gallium looked from her to Princess Opal and cleared his throat. "Well, we'd better take our seats." Tugging on her hand, they bowed to the royal family again before leaving to join his parents seated in the crowd.

Princess Opal watched them walk away. "Did you enjoy discussing her wedding gown in front of me?" she whispered.

King Carlomon sighed. "I didn't do it to slight you. Gallium was obviously upset about your sister's passing. I only wanted to give him a bit of comfort."

"Comfort? At my expense? It's bad enough she's hanging all over him like cheap fabric, but you making her think she's important when she's not doesn't make me feel any better. Sometimes I wonder why I even returned to Coldarius. You've always overlooked me for Dellah. Maybe you feel the wrong daughter died."

Princess Revari squirmed uncomfortably in her arms.

"That's a terrible thing to say," admonished King Carlomon. "It's also untrue. I'm glad we're standing where no one can hear you. Today isn't about you—it's about Dellah. I'm being forced to bury my young daughter and watch *her* daughters grow up without her. All of us are distraught over Dellah's death, but we have a duty to the princesses. This is no time for pettiness and jealousy."

She checked the room before responding, keeping her face neutral as though not to draw attention. "Are you saying I'm jealous of Legend Guilde?"

He bowed his head. "I don't have the strength to fight with you. Not today. Let's just get through the day for Dellah and her daughters' sake. All right?"

"I'll get through it just fine," she said evenly. "But if you think I'm jealous of some poor commoner, I have news for you. She isn't half the WomanForm I am!"

Noting Lady Alarah watching from a distance, he moved in front of Princess Opal to block her view. "I won't let you turn a celebration of your sister's life into an excerpt of a petty schoolgirl's journal entry. I'm telling you—get it together. If you plan on being a mother figure to your nieces, you'd better carry yourself with the grace and dignity your sister had. I won't have you acting like Lady Alarah."

Concentrating on Princess Revari prevented her from raising her voice. "First you say I'm jealous of a commoner, and now I'm emulating Lady Alarah? You're really piling up the insults, aren't you? Don't worry, Father. I'll be sure not to do anything that'll bring shame to your precious reputation. I can't believe you'd turn on me for someone like her."

He placed his hands on her shoulders. "I'd never turn on you for anyone. I love you. You and my granddaughters are all I have left. I'm asking you to please let go of this fantasy you have of Gallium. For me? He doesn't want you, Opal. It's only going to make you more miserable than you are now."

She adjusted the princess's gown. "The only one making me miserable is you. Right now, the only thing that would make me happier is getting as far away from you as possible."

She forced a bright smile on her face and repositioned the baby before leaving him to wonder how he'd lost control of the situation. Sending her to Earth hadn't solved anything. Her heart was as hard as ever. He prayed to The One to give him strength. He'd already lost one daughter. He didn't know what he'd do if he lost another.

Lady Alarah inhaled the luxurious scent of the blue rose she'd stolen from the queen's death craft. Adding it to the large bundle she'd hidden in her bag, she thought, *It seems I got my hands on your roses after all, huh, Dellah? Didn't you say it would be over your dead body before I'd have them?*

She smiled evilly at Queen Dellah.

No one is more happier than I am to finally see you dead.

From what she could gather, things weren't as peaceful in the royal household. She nodded to a few Beings she recognized as she sampled delicacies from the buffet tables. She'd thoroughly enjoyed watching the uncomfortable exchange between Legend and Princess Opal.

But what was most intriguing were the dynamics that unfolded between the princess and her father. While the other parishioners were focused on Queen Dellah, she had kept her attention on them.

Addicted to gossip and blackmail, over time, reading lips had become a specialty of hers. From where she sat, she could see everything the king and his daughter had discussed.

So Princess Opal is in love with Gallium and despises Legend Guilde. How interesting.

Smiling to herself, she placed a few crab puffs on her plate and poured a generous amount of butter on a lobster tail. Coldarius's oceans and lakes produced the best seafood. Hearing of the queen's death had been the highlight of her week, but watching her father suffer had set her on a permanent high.

She intended to eat her fill with gusto. She spied Legend sitting and talking with her mother and Gallium's family. Since the fate of Platirius was up in arms, it would be beneficial to form alliances. She plotted how to turn the situation around to suit her ambitious nature.

Alliances, she'd learned, were the key to prosperity. Now that Queen Dellah was rotting away, numerous doors of opportunity had opened to her. She intended to walk through every last one of them.

King Carlomon closed the door on the massive gate located a short distance from the palace. His daughter had been laid to rest with her mother, Queen Elia, his brother, Prince Bocham, and his mother and father, the former queen and king of Coldarius. He placed his head up against the cool stone wall of the mausoleum.

She'd been much too young to die. He wished he'd been taken in her place. No parent wanted their ChildForms to go before them. He wanted to rant and rave—to question why the One would be so cruel. Yet, he held tightly to his emotions. His community needed him—he couldn't afford to lose control.

He tried to take comfort in believing his beloved daughter was safe with their loved ones in the Afterlife. Princess Revari cried loudly as the death bells tolled on—signaling the end of the incredible life of the formidable Queen Dellah.

Princess Vivant stood staring at the door of the mausoleum. If it were possible, she would've healed her mother and brought her home. Rivers of tears silently flowed down her cheeks. She was angry with everyone—about everything. The bells were too loud and her sister wouldn't stop crying. It was too cold and she didn't like her hair.

Although her aunt had styled it into a fashionable look, she could never emulate her mother's graceful style. She fought down a surge of anger. Why did she have to die? Why couldn't it have been someone else's mother? Her gaze found Lady Alarah, who was failing miserably at hiding a self-satisfied grin.

The One should've taken *her* instead of her mother. She knew her thoughts were selfish, but she didn't care. Her mother had been the most powerful WomanForm in the universe. It wasn't fair The One had snatched her away from her and her sister.

Didn't He have enough Beings within His realm to keep Him company? He had no reason to ask her mother to leave them behind. She looked over at Princess Revari, who was still wailing loudly.

She took her from Princess Opal. Lifting her onto her shoulder, she patted her on the back. Princess Revari hiccupped and looked at her.

"You're sleepy," she told her. "We're going back to Grandfather's palace soon. Mother isn't coming with us, and Grandfather says Father has lost his mind. Maybe you and I will go home to Platirius when he gets better. Would you like that, baby Revari?" The baby's cries grew louder.

Gallium knelt beside her. "Let me try to get her to sleep, Princess Vivant. Please?"

She looked up at the handsome MaleForm and handed her sister over to him. Immediately, her cries stopped.

He rocked her gently as the Chief Minister said the final prayer for Queen Dellah. When she sighed and fell asleep on his shoulder, Gallium smiled down at Princess Vivant.

"Everything is going to be all right, Princess Vivant. I won't let anything happen to you or your sister. Do you remember me?"

She nodded. "You're my mother's friend. She says I should always be nice to you because you were loyal to her. And...you're the only one who'll understand about my secret."

He cocked his head curiously. "What secret?"

Her silver eyes, reminiscent of her mother's, carefully searched his face. "The secret I'm never supposed to share with anyone—not even my father. I can't tell you now. But when something gets sick, I'll show you."

He blinked and stared down at her. "Ah...okay."

"But you can't tell anyone. If you do, Father will lock me away in the Chamber of Despair."

His eyes hardening, he kneeled to her. "I want you to listen to me very carefully. No one is going to lock you away anywhere. Do you understand? I'm here to protect both of you."

She sniffed and nodded. "That's what Mother said. She said you promised you'd keep me and baby Revari safe."

Smiling through his tears, he said, "I did, and I was happy to do it. Don't worry about anything. You're going to be just fine."

"Thank you." Turning her attention back to the Chief Minister, she asked, "Is it cold where Mother is?"

"No," he stated gently.

"Will she be hungry? Is there enough food in The One's dining chamber for her? She likes to eat cookies after bedtime."

He smiled and looked up at the sky before he answered. He hadn't expected her innocent questions to affect him so deeply. "Your mother will never be hungry or cold ever again. She's living a good life just as she did when she was here with us."

"Then why couldn't we go with her? Didn't she love us anymore?"

He shook his head sadly. "Oh no. It wasn't that at all. I don't know why she was taken from us, but she loved you and your sister very much. We won't understand until we meet her again in the Afterlife."

Princess Revari stirred. Instinctively, he gently patted her on the back. "Please understand, she never wanted to leave you. When The One called her away, she had to go. We don't have a choice in things like this."

She frowned. "I hate The One. He destroyed my family."

He was at a loss about what to say to make her feel better. How could he explain death to her when he didn't understand it either?

King Carlomon signaled it was time for them to throw roses at the door of the burial chamber. He shifted Princess Revari in his arms and extended his hand to Princess Vivant. The grand DeathCeremony for Queen Dellah had ended. It was time to go home.

Chapter 3

"The princesses are sleeping soundly in their beds," announced Princess Opal. "It's been a long day."

Gallium watched her descend the spiral staircase before looking out the expansive window at the stars. The largest one winked at him.

"The longest. My heart breaks for Princess Vivant. Princess Revari won't remember her, but she's old enough to feel her loss. She's never going to forget her mother."

She joined him at the window and looked up into the beautiful star-filled night. "None of us will. She was a force to be reckoned with. How can anyone forget someone as beautiful and powerful as her?" She turned to him. "I had the staff prepare a room for you to sleep in. Surely you're not going to go out into such a cold night as this?"

He shook his head. "No, I need to get home. My cottage is just a little ways from the palace. It won't take me long to reach it."

You're not getting away from me tonight. "But what if Princess Vivant wakes up and wants to talk to you? What do I do? You handled her so well at the burial. She'll need you now more than ever."

He ducked his head, embarrassed by her show of appreciation. "I know, and I'll be here for her and her sister."

He sighed. "I'm not an expert on InfantForms and ChildForms."

She smiled up at him. "You have just as much experience with them as I do—next to none. But I'm confident you'll do your best. That's more than I can ask of you."

He looked down at her. "Everyone says it's difficult to tell you apart, but I don't think so. I could never confuse you with Queen Dellah."

She tilted her head toward him. "Oh? Is that bad?"

"Not at all. You have your own style and a different perspective on life. You're hesitant while she was confident in making decisions. She took charge, but you're content to follow. You show vulnerability—she didn't."

He looked out of the window again. "None of it is bad—it's just different." He sighed heavily. "One of the best lessons she taught me was there's nothing wrong with being different."

He missed the look of longing in her eyes. His words were sweet music to her ears. She'd been afraid he'd want her to act like her sister and was pleased to find that wasn't true. He accepted her for who she was and all that she had to give.

She wanted him to take her in his arms and kiss her fears away. But it couldn't happen yet. Not with Legend in her way. The sooner she found a way to get rid of her, the better off all of them would be.

She slipped her hands into his. It made her happy he didn't pull away from her. Hand in hand, they stood together, silently watching the stars.

K ing Micah flew into Platirius from Maieman to pay his condolences on the loss of Queen Dellah. He stood looking around in awe at the emptiness of the expansive courtyards. A soldier casually strode by, whistling a melancholy tune. At the sight of the king, he stopped and bowed.

"Excuse me. Could you tell me where I might find King Dubian?"

The soldier scratched his head. "I—uh. King Dubian? He's in the Chamber of Despair."

He nodded. "I see. He's overseeing some affairs?"

The soldier looked at him sheepishly and shook his head. "Well, he's... They locked him up in there."

"He's locked away? On whose authority?"

"Well...he flipped out after Queen Dellah died. He kept claiming she was still alive, so King Carlomon had him locked up. It's funny though, because there's a lady who looks just like her."

King Micah leaned forward eagerly. "Yes, that's Princess Opal, Queen Dellah's twin sister."

"Uh...yeah. Well, she left with the rest of the Coldarians. King Dubian has been asking if she'll come back, but we don't know what to tell him. He's not the same anymore. They took Queen Dellah away too. I heard she was buried on Coldarius."

He briefly closed his eyes. "Where's my son?"

"Major Kron? He's not here. He just won against King Hitam."

He tried to hold onto what was left of his patience. Trying to get answers from the soldier was akin to pulling teeth. He was a BrainStaff without power—or a brain.

"I'm aware of that, but I thought he'd be back by now."

The soldier looked over his shoulder. "There he is," he said, pointing across the courtyard.

He turned to see Major Kron marching toward him with hundreds of soldiers in tow. Sighing in relief, he said, "Thank you, soldier. You may report to your station."

The soldier saluted him. "Thank you, King Micah."

Major Kron embraced him warmly. "Father? What are you doing here?"

"I came to see how King Dubian was faring, but I've just been informed he's in the Chamber of Despair. King Carlomon ordered him to be locked away."

Major Kron raised an eyebrow. "Has he overthrown Platirius? Is he in charge now?"

"No. That's what makes it so perplexing. It seems the Coldarians have abandoned Platirius. No one is running anything."

Major Kron turned to the soldiers. "I want fifty of you guarding King Dubian. The rest can be stationed inside the palace and the work chambers."

The surprised soldiers looked from him to King Micah. "Go and do as I say!" he roared.

The soldiers saluted him and hurried away to their posts.

"Why did King Carlomon have him locked up?"

King Micah let out a deep sigh. "Queen Dellah is dead. She passed while giving birth. Apparently, it drove him mad. While I understand King Carlomon did what he felt was necessary, I don't understand why he didn't finish him off and take Platirius."

"By The One—what a tragedy. I know he loved her very much, so I'm not surprised he took her death hard." He rubbed his hand across his growing beard. "We have to get him out of there. You're a king, they'll listen to you. Once he's released, he can go back to performing his duties."

King Micah held out a hand to stop him. "Now wait a minute, Lucian, let's not be so hasty. Maybe it'll be better with him out of the way. You've won a great victory for Platirius."

Looking around carefully, he lowered his voice to a whisper. "If you're appointed to general, you could take over for him and get the military under your command. Then...if he's better—and that may be a big if—he can be freed down the road."

"Don't we need him to be free to make the appointment?"

"No, I can do it. Look at the state of this place. Even with those you brought back from Kikhani, you still have less troops than Coldarius. Let me help you rebuild the army with conscripts from home and our allies. If you learned anything from Queen Dellah, it's that the one who controls the military is the real power behind a kingdom."

King Micah gave a reproachful look when he hesitated. "I understand we reared you to be loyal to authority, but you must think about yourself now. He's not well-liked. It's only a matter of time before someone comes to claim the throne. Why shouldn't it be you? You've done all the grunt work. A win against King Hitam was no small feat."

"You're right, but in the eyes of many, I'm still a ChildForm." He removed his hat and wiped his brow before putting it back on. "Before I left for Kikhani, they didn't like or respect me."

King Micah's steely gaze was confident. "They will now. You're just what Platirius needs. It's possible to take control of this kingdom, but you must start now, son. You'd be a much better king than he'll ever be."

He placed his hands on his son's broad shoulders. "You're smarter, stronger, and faster. Unlike him, you know how to take control of the soldiers. Opportunities like this don't come often, so you have to reach out and take them."

"I respect King Dubian, but I don't think he'll ever measure up to be the king you are." He scanned the small group of MaleForms half-heartedly trying to assume the tasks the

WomenForms did. "You're right. It's time I started rebuilding Platirius."

"That's the spirit! Platirius could be yours, son. I'm so proud of you. Come! Let's see to your appointment—General Kron."

He smiled broadly. "That's the best news I've heard all day."

K ing Micah gathered everyone inside the worship chamber to witness the promotion. Major Kron had expected the Platirians not to support him. To his surprise, they'd grown weary of King Dubian's antics.

Now that one of his loudest supporters, Sergeant Fontine, was dead, they were eager to get rid of him. Loud cheers rang out as Major Kron became General Kron.

He stood at the podium with pride shining in his eyes. "Thank you all for sharing this prestigious honor with me. We all know Platirius is one of the greatest empires in the galaxy."

Adjusting the microphone, he said, "Since I was a ChildForm, I've heard of the epic battles fought and won by the former kings. To let its glory end would be a disgrace. I intend to bring respect and prosperity back to it!"

The halls thundered with roars of support for their new leader. But he hadn't won over everyone. More than a few of King Dubian's supporters subtly murmured their displeasure.

"When will King Dubian be released from the Chamber of Despair?" asked Chief Counselor Garoni.

Silence descended over the crowd when the oldest member of the justice council approached the podium.

"Never in Platirius's history has a king been locked away in his own mental chamber. He's been unjustly imprisoned—without even a trial. Would you say that's fair to him, General Kron? After all, he's the son of King Anemi, not you."

He nodded toward King Micah. "What gives your father the right to take away his birthright and hand it to you?"

An uneasiness shifted among the MaleForms. Chief Counselor Garoni focused his attention on them. "Platirius's throne has always passed within the bloodlines. King Dubian is a second-born son, but he's still royalty. How are we comfortable with watching an outsider steal the throne for himself?"

"That's not what my son is trying to do—" said King Micah.

The Chief Counselor's eyes narrowed. "That's exactly what he's trying to do," he said coldly. "He hasn't been on Platirius for a year, and isn't old enough to shave, yet you believe he should take charge of our planet?"

He pointed his staff at King Micah. "If you want him to govern a kingdom, then speed up your death and have him take your place on Maieman. We won't sit by and watch this treasonous act bear fruit."

General Kron could feel his support dwindling under the weight of the Chief Counselor's influence. He placed his hand on King Micah's arm to prevent him from attacking the Chief Counselor.

The elder MaleForm glared balefully at him. "What do you say, General Kron? Shall we bring you before the justice council to convince us this isn't treason? I'll warn you, if you lose your case, you'll be thrown into the Flames of Justice."

He smirked at King Micah before shifting his eyes to the young general. "Of course, that could be avoided if King Dubian were released today. Then we can all get back to normal."

General Kron looked over the seven MaleForm members of the justice council and the Platirian soldiers. The Maieman troops were tense and ready to strike at his command. If the soldiers turned on each other, chaos would ensue, and order would never be properly restored.

"Father, I don't think I have a choice. I can't risk a revolt."

"But, Lucian—"

"It won't change anything. You're right—the true power of a planet rests on the strength of its military. We have many of our Maieman soldiers supporting us and will be dispatched soon. I can still assume control of the military. Let's let them think they have the upper hand by releasing him."

King Micah gave the Chief Counselor a withering glance. "And if his lunacy destroys this place?"

"Then I can always come home. I'll make a name for myself—with or without the king's demise."

"I'll support whatever decision you make. Just promise me if things get too difficult, you'll come home."

"Of course, but I don't think it's going to come to that. I have a feeling someone will put King Dubian out of his misery. Then? Platirius will never be the same."

General Kron turned to face the crowd. "Your request will be granted. King Dubian will be released from the Chamber of Despair today. But know this, Chief Counselor Garoni, I'm the commander of this army and always will be. Every soldier here will follow my orders or they'll face execution."

The Chief Counselor's black eyes raked over his face. "A bold proclamation, General. Your cockiness stems from knowing our king is at your mercy because he needs an army to protect what's left of Platirius. You should pray to The One your luck doesn't run out."

"Luck has nothing to do with it. Everyone here is safe because of me. I could've lost my life on Kikhani and none of you would've cared."

"That's right," said King Micah. "My son saved all of you. The least you can do is show him respect."

Chief Counselor Garoni smiled and pivoted on his heel. His work was finished—for the moment. King Micah and General Kron watched as he approached the justice chamber.

"He's going to be trouble," said King Micah.

"I know," said General Kron, his eyes trained on the Chief Counselor's back. "But if he crosses me, I'll find a way to get rid of him. I'm finally rising to the top. By the hand of The One, none of the Platirians will get in my way."

L egend came running toward the back of the store. "Sinae Swift, I told you not to play in those plants! What have you gotten into?"

Sinae's cries could be heard all the way in front of the store where she'd been ringing up customers. "I picked a CallePepper bulb! It was so pretty, but I rubbed my eyes, and now they're burning! I can't see, Legend!"

She groaned. "How many times have I told you plants aren't toys? Come with me."

She ushered her to the water station and bathed her eyes in cool water. Sinae flinched as the spicy CallePepper mixed with the water, draining down the corners of her eyes.

Gallium entered the store and set down a large box of seedlings. "I heard screaming. What's the matter?"

She rolled her eyes. "Now do you see why I don't want ChildForms?"

He grinned. "Not all ChildForms are alike, you know?"

She assisted Sinae to stand and patted her face with a cool towel. "No, I don't know, nor do I want to."

He leaned against the water station. "Not even if our ChildForms look like me?" he teased.

"Go outside and play, Sinae." She tossed a clean towel at him. "The sun rises and sets on your face, but don't push your luck, General Barrios!"

He plucked a budding rose from a bush and placed it in her hair. "Well, I guess I'll have to find a way to change your mind."

She folded her arms. "I hear Princess Opal would love to make you a father."

His cheerful mood vanished in a flash. "Listen, let's not go there. She's no more in love with me than I am with her."

She wasn't convinced. "I see the way she looks at you. Everyone can see it except you."

He lifted his hands in the air. "She just lost her sister and is raising her nieces—that's a tough job for anyone, royalty or not. The last thing on her mind is me! Legend, you're overreacting. I came to treat you to luncheon, not to talk about her!"

She pouted. She hadn't meant to bring her up, but she didn't like hearing he'd spent the night at the palace after the DeathCeremony.

Princess Opal had looked too pleased with herself when she casually discussed it within earshot of her. She was convinced she'd done it on purpose to anger her.

He tried to salvage the good vibes. "You're so cute when you pout."

"Yes, I'm cute. I'm also hungry, so let us go. Just so you know, since you're on King Carlomon's payroll, I expect to be treated to the most expensive dishes on the menu."

He was relieved she'd dropped discussing Princess Opal so quickly. "Done. Nothing is too good for my future bride."

She turned around for him to assist her in putting on her coat. "I'll make sure you never forget that."

He kissed her soft lips. "I don't intend to."

Hearing the door chime, she expelled a breath. "I forgot to put up the *Closed* sign."

"It's okay. I'll let whomever is out there know you're on luncheon leave." He took her hand in his. "Come with me, almost Mrs. Barrios."

She grinned at him as they walked toward the front of the store, holding hands. Her joy died on her lips when she saw who was waiting. Gripping his hand tightly, she forced herself to remain calm.

"Oh, hello, Gallium. I didn't expect to find you here. I came to pick up an order for my father," said Princess Opal.

Legend noted she had completely ignored her. Again.

Gently disengaging her hand from his, she said, "King Carlomon orders two bouquets of white roses every week," she told Gallium. "One moment, Princess Opal. I'll get them."

Princess Opal barely glanced at her. "So he still places flowers in front of my mother's crypt? Wow. After all this time, I thought he would've stopped."

Legend retrieved the beautiful arrangements of roses and handed them to her. "I think it's very generous to never forget the ones you love. You're very lucky to have him for a FatherForm."

"What was yours like?" she asked suddenly.

Legend's mouth opened, clearly taken aback by the question. "Oh, well, let's see. I was in my fourth lifespan when he died. I don't remember much of him except he loved planting flowers."

She looked around the shop. "He and my mother opened this place together. I think she keeps it going to keep his memory alive."

He squeezed her hand. "I think that's wonderful. Maybe that's what drew you to me."

She smiled at him. "I never thought of it that way, but I think you may be right. I think most WomenForms want to be with someone like their FatherForms."

"Do you think he would've approved of me?"

She lifted his large hand to her cheek. "I know he would have. I can imagine you and him spending most of your time talking about plants and digging around in the dirt."

They smiled at each other. Princess Opal barely refrained from rolling her eyes. "Who wouldn't approve of you, Gallium?" she said sweetly. "You're our hero. There's not a braver or stronger MaleForm I know besides my father."

He blushed. "I—um, thank you, Princess Opal."

She cradled the roses to her breasts, beaming up at him. "It's my pleasure. Oh, Gallium, Princess Revari does the cutest thing! She purses her lips when she's hungry!"

His smile widened. "Really? That's amazing! She's growing so fast."

"Yes, she is! You should come to the palace and see her. I know she'd love that. And Princess Vivant too."

He nodded. "Er... Sure, I'd love to see them again."

Legend noted the strange way Princess Opal was looking at him. "I don't want her to forget a detail of your face. I certainly haven't."

An uncomfortable silence permeated the room. "Well, I'd better get these back to the palace. I don't want to keep Father waiting. Gallium, when will you be available to see the princesses?"

He paused and looked at Legend. Her expressionless face held its peace. "I can stop by this evening on my way home if that's okay."

Princess Opal's smile was a mirror image of Queen Dellah's. "Perfect! I'll tell the dining staff to prepare a good supper, but I won't tell Princess Vivant. She's been so down lately. She needs a good surprise to cheer her up. In a while, Gallium."

Legend glared at the closed door, shaking her head. "In a while, Gallium!" she said, mocking her. "She acted as if I wasn't standing here—what a piece of work!"

He pivoted to her. "Come on, Legend. That's not fair."

She placed her hand on her hip. "Not fair? Did you hear her? She certainly hasn't forgotten a detail of your face? I assume she means when she was on Earth? Sorry, but that's just creepy!"

"You're being unkind. Sure, she's different than Queen Dellah, but—"

"Oh, she's nothing like Queen Dellah! The queen was no-nonsense and in your face. She said what she meant and stood by it. Princess Opal is the epitome of passive-aggressive.

She practically threw herself at you while barely saying a word to me!"

He reflected on Princess Opal's words. "She asked about your father. I think that's a sign she's trying to get to know you."

She couldn't believe he was so blind. "No, she wasn't. I don't know why she asked about him, but it definitely wasn't to build rapport with me. She doesn't like me. And what's worse, I think she's using the princesses to get closer to you!"

She hit a nerve mentioning the princesses. "Stop. They're her nieces and she loves them. She wouldn't use them to put herself in a good light with me or anyone else."

She let out an exasperated sigh. "She's in love with you! You don't see that?"

He felt himself losing patience. "Will you please stop spouting this nonsense? She doesn't have feelings for me! I keep telling you, she's trying to adjust to losing her sister. She's doing the best she can with a terrible situation that none of us asked for. Why can't you muster some form of sympathy for her?"

"Because I don't like her!" she shouted.

"Why?" He hadn't meant to elevate his voice, but he couldn't help it. "She hasn't done anything to make you dislike her."

She couldn't believe he was being so thick-headed. "How about trying to steal my fiancé? Is that a good enough reason?"

He threw back his head and laughed. "No one can steal me from you." He grabbed her hand. "Baby, I'm where I want to be. There's no reason to be jealous of her."

She snatched her hand away. "I'm not jealous of her! She's sneaky and mean-spirited. The only reason you can't see it is because she has Queen Dellah's face. But she doesn't have her heart. Queen Dellah was kind and giving, but Princess Opal?" She tapped her manicured fingernail on the crystal counter. "She's about as transparent as this."

He rubbed his eyes. "Since she returned, we've argued a lot more than we've made up. I don't understand why you're doing this. You know I'm loyal to you and I'd cut off my right arm before I'd hurt you. What do I have to say to convince you that you have nothing to worry about?"

She crossed her arms over her breasts. "I'm not doing anything. It's her! And I can't believe you're blaming me for telling you the truth. You've always listened to me before. Why can't you see what she's doing?"

The chill in his eyes sank her heart. "She walked in here to buy flowers. She made polite conversation and asked about your father. What am I too dumb to see? Please spell it out for me as if I'm a ChildForm."

"Oh, Gallium," she said sadly. "I don't think you're stupid. But you're blind. You're blind to her antics because you miss Queen Dellah. We all miss her. But she's not Queen Dellah and she never will be."

"I've never tried to replace my friend, and I wish you'd stop using her memory in whatever imaginary vendetta you have against her sister," he snapped. "Princess Opal is a part of the royal family that governs us. She deserves your respect."

She backed away from him. "I give respect where it's due. She hasn't shown me an ounce of it since she came. I understand my place, but I'm certainly not about to allow her to spit on me as if I'm garbage!"

"She's not spitting on you! That's your insecurity rearing again!" He threw his hands up in the air. "Look, we're not getting anywhere with this. We've spent half of my luncheon time arguing over nothing! I'll go to the dining chamber and pick you up a sandwich and some soup. Then I need to get back to work."

"Oh, don't trouble yourself. I'll eat with my mother. Why don't you use your remaining time to eat with Princess Opal? I'm sure she'd *love* to have you."

They stared at each other in silence. He shook his head and left without a word. Finally, she allowed her tears to fall. For many reasons, she wished Queen Dellah hadn't died. Then maybe she never would've met her sister. The princesses were without a mother. That meant she wouldn't return to Earth anytime soon.

She'd been raised to be a strong WomanForm—to see past illusions and pettiness. But something about Princess Opal made her uneasy. Before she arrived, Gallium had always listened to her. Now they couldn't be in the same room without arguing. Just when she'd found someone to love and to return her love, she feared she'd lose it all.

Mrs. Guilde quietly brought out bowls of clam chowder, brioche rolls, thick sandwiches made with chopped fish, chives, and scallions in a tangy sauce, and tall mugs of hot apple cider.

She carefully set the food on the small table facing the window before turning to rub Legend's back.

"Oh, Mother!" she cried, wiping her tears. "I didn't know you heard us."

"Don't cry, Legend," she pleaded. "Gallium loves you. He's not going anywhere."

"Mother, am I crazy? Am I wrong about what I'm seeing? Maybe I am insecure and jealous of her because she's a gorgeous princess. I didn't feel this way about Queen Dellah, so why does she irritate me? Maybe he's right. Maybe I'm the problem."

"No," said Mrs. Guilde darkly. "You are spot on about Princess Opal. Her heart is as wicked as Lady Alarah's and always has been. Come and sit with me."

Sobbing, she allowed herself to be led to the table. Mrs. Guilde handed her a silk napkin and sat down. Legend sat and soundly blew her nose.

Mrs. Guilde nodded toward her bowl. "Eat your chowder. Mr. Poppol caught the clams fresh this morning. I put lots of them and fresh cream in the chowder for you."

She groaned. "I'm too upset to eat, Mother."

"We're not going to waste good food over that scheming WomanForm," said Mrs. Guilde. "You don't know why King Carlomon sent her to Earth, but I do."

Legend's head snapped up. "I thought she was there to complete missions about the Humans?"

Mrs. Guilde nodded. "She was, but that's only part of it. Have you ever heard of a king sending his daughter to another planet—and Earth at that?"

She thought for a moment. "Well...no, but I hear she's a good spy."

Mrs. Guilde stared at her. "Why do you think that is, Legend?"

She stirred her spoon into the bowl. "I honestly don't know anything about her."

Mrs. Guilde bit into her sandwich and chewed. "To be a spy, you have to have a sneaky, dubious spirit. You were away at school when King Carlomon sent her away. I thought she would get over her obsession with young MaleForms, but it appears she hasn't."

She blinked. "What are you talking about?"

Mrs. Guilde looked up at her. "Legend, WomenForms have a sixth sense about other WomenForms. MaleForms are blind when it comes to the tricks they pull, but we aren't. As I said, you aren't wrong about her. The reason King Carlomon sent her to Earth was..." Her voice trailed off.

Legend waited. "Please tell me, Mother. Is Gallium in danger?"

"No, but you are. She feels you're in her way and that makes her just as dangerous as ever. She had to leave Coldarius because of the wicked things she did when she was younger. Dellah was always the headstrong one of the two, but her sister has always been...odd."

She passed Legend the piping hot bowl of rolls. "Dellah made friends easily, but Opal never learned how to socialize properly with others. If she felt her peers didn't like her—whether it was true or just in her mind—she made sure their ParentForms punished them in front of her. That ostracized her even more."

Removing her spoon from the silk napkin, she said, "Dellah was well-liked, but the other ChildForms steered clear of Opal. Then...she became obsessed with a young MaleForm who looked a lot like Gallium."

She took a sip of cider. "This has BorborWine in it. Drink it slowly. I'll need it to get through this story, and you need it to calm down. Strange things began happening—things we'd never seen before. Coldarius has always been small and peaceful until Opal started becoming a WomanForm."

Legend let the smooth, hot liquid travel down her throat. It warmed her from the inside.

"She was fixated on the young MaleForm. He couldn't breathe without her forcing her attention on him. Then, the female ChildForm he was fond of became gravely ill."

Snow began to fall heavily as she recounted the gruesome details of Princess Opal's past. "She started vomiting out of the blue and spent many weeks in the medical chamber before she was able to return home. We thought that would be the end of it, but strange accidents started happening."

Legend's hand stilled on the cup. She hadn't realized she was holding her breath.

"Then, her brother died. He was poisoned. Her sister was the next to die. She was found sprawled out at the bottom of the mountain. Pretty soon, the ParentForms were dead too."

Mrs. Guilde paused to take another sip of cider. "All of her family members ended up dead and no one knew why. Finally, Princess Opal's rival died too. She was found locked in a freezer in the old dining chamber. King Carlomon had it demolished and rebuilt, but by then, the entire family had perished."

Legend's mouth dropped, but Mrs. Guilde continued.

"It was rumored that the male ChildForm began to suspect her when she said something strange to him. He told his MotherForm that she asked him if he felt better that the female and her family were gone."

She refilled Legend's glass. "Then one night, he disappeared. His ParentForms were frantic. They begged King Carlomon to find him—he was their only ChildForm. He was found hanging in one of the wine chambers under the palace. His body was mangled as if he had been beaten. The soldiers found him covered in bruises."

Legend's stomach was twisting into knots. The creepy feeling she got when Princess Opal was around wasn't just in her head. She leaned forward to listen.

"When the royal guards questioned her, she acted as if she didn't know him. But they found his school identification in her room. And belongings of the female ChildForm and her family."

Mrs. Guilde's golden eyes were sad. "She had a souvenir from each of them—hair ribbons, an apron, a watch, and a single knitted sock. When the brother was found, he was only wearing one sock. The one they found in her room was a perfect match."

Mrs. Guilde cut into her sandwich. "Eat up. You'll need strength to hear all of this. She chased that young MaleForm all over Coldarius, wanting to win his affection. She never did. He knew she was strange."

The snow fell and melted on the windows as Legend listened to her mother's soothing voice. "After he died, she erased him from her memory like data in a computer. By then, she had set her sights on Gallium. But Gallium was into sports and his plants. He didn't make time for females."

Legend broke off a piece of the bread and dipped it into the chowder. Her first bite was delicious. She dipped another piece into the bowl. Her mother made excellent chowder, but hearing about Princess Opal's twisted past nearly ruined her appetite.

"By The One, Mother. Did she kill all those Beings by herself?"

"I believe she did, but there was no way King Carlomon and Queen Elia would allow their daughter to stand before our justice council and be judged for it. They sent her away. I believe it broke Queen Elia's heart. She died soon after she left."

Mrs Guilde ladled another portion of chowder into her bowl. "She kept her dirty deeds from Dellah, too, because she knew she would've stopped her. In the end, she was left to pick up the pieces. Thankfully, no one blamed her for her sister's craziness."

"No wonder she was so strong," murmured Legend. She sat up straight. "Oh no! Gallium!"

"Is a MaleForm," interjected Mrs. Guilde, "and can handle his own against her if and when the time comes. You needn't worry about him. He has a special ability he's had since birth. She won't be able to kill him easily, if at all."

"Had it not been for Queen Dellah dying, she never would've returned to Coldarius."

"Probably not. It was the only time I lost a bit of respect for King Carlomon and Queen Elia. Six Beings died due to her insanity. I was privy to the information because your father, Gallium's mother, and I worked in the palace then."

Dusting crumbs into the bread basket, she said, "No one else found out. King Carlomon made sure it was swept under the rug to protect his daughter. But it wasn't fair. She had no right to take their lives and go free."

Legend thought of something. "Mother? Is she aware you know about her?"

"No. She knows your father knew because King Carlomon ordered him to bury the bodies so that no one would find them. I never crossed paths with the little monster."

"So that's why she asked about my father. Did she think he'd shared this with me?"

Mrs. Guilde wiped her hands on her napkin. "Who knows what goes on in that warped mind of hers? I know she doesn't like you. But it's not because of what happened in the past. It's about what's happening now. I doubt she even remembers those poor souls. She wants Gallium, and she'll pull every string possible to get rid of you."

She caught Legend's arm as she stood to clear away the dishes. "But this time, I won't sit by and allow her to harm you. You're right about her using the princesses to get close to him."

Her grip instinctively tightened. "Every second those ChildForms are in her care, they're in danger. If she assumes her sister's role in their lives, at least one or both of them will grow up to be just like her." Mrs. Guilde shuddered. "May The One help us all if that happens."

"Do you think she's murdered any Humans?" asked Legend.

"I wouldn't doubt it. Think about it. Who would stop her? Now she's back here and she knows she's untouchable."

"Well, we'll have to find a way to deal with her. Everyone was focused on King Dubian going crazy, and here we have a serial killer living among us. Those poor little princesses deserve so much better than him and Princess Opal." She straightened a pin on her mother's blouse. "Do you think I should tell Gallium about her?"

Mrs. Guilde shook her head. "No, don't tell him anything. He'll think you're trying to dig up dirt on her. Etienne knows about her too. Let him hear it from her. He'll listen to his mother better than you, and that'll put him on guard about protecting the princesses."

She sighed. "If something happens to King Carlomon and her, are you prepared to take on the responsibility of rearing two ChildForms? I understand you've never wanted to be a MotherForm because you want to focus on your career. It would be a huge sacrifice."

"I honestly haven't thought about it. Moving up the ranks means everything to me. I don't know if I'd choose the princesses over my career."

"Or Gallium, if he chose to raise them?"

She looked away. Mrs. Guilde patted her arm and stood. "It's all right. I've placed a lot on your shoulders. Let's see how it all plays out. I'm going up to take a nap. Keep the shop closed for the rest of the day. There's no need to worry about things we can't control."

Legend cleared the dishes and entered them into the high-powered sanitizer. She didn't want to think about the possibility of losing Gallium, but she also didn't know if she could help him shoulder the responsibility of ChildForms she hadn't borne.

And what of King Dubian? What if he issued a challenge to King Carlomon for his daughters? She hoped she'd never have to find out.

Chapter 4

G allium placed the last of the equipment into the cupboard and closed it soundly. His neck was tense from all the work he'd done, but he needed to let off a bit of steam. As long as he had breath, he'd never understand why WomenForms couldn't get along with each other.

Until Princess Opal returned, Legend had been fun and easy going. Now her suspicion of the princess had nearly become an obsession. Princess Opal hadn't made him suspect she'd been anything except gracious and kind. He couldn't understand why Legend was so bothered by her.

Was it jealousy? There certainly was no need for that. In his eyes, she was the most captivating Being he'd ever seen and always would be. He tried to reach her again, but the transmission was still on read.

They didn't have antiquated, physical phones like Humans. All communications, personal or business, were sent on their palms. So there was no excuse why she wasn't answering.

It wasn't hard to believe she was deliberately ignoring his calls. He ran his fingers through his thick hair. Maybe he should cut it.

But she liked his hair long. If he cut it, would that start another argument? He hoped not. He didn't like being at odds with her.

On the other hand, if he kept his distance from the palace, that meant he wouldn't get to see the princesses. That wasn't an option. He loved Legend, but he needed the princesses as much as they needed him.

Especially Princess Revari. Her young life had begun so unfairly. He wanted to do what he could to make things easier for her.

Legend was wrong. He was fully aware Princess Opal shared Queen Dellah's face, but she wasn't her. Not by a long shot. He'd never confused that fact. She didn't have her confidence or fire, and she depended on MaleForms to make all of the decisions.

While that wouldn't have bothered him before moving to Platirius, he'd become accustomed to Queen Dellah's take-charge personality.

After seeing her wield power, he realized he wouldn't be happy with a WomanForm who never challenged him. He was drawn to spirited souls, not doormats. He'd never thought of Princess Opal as anything more than King Carlomon's daughter.

He wished Legend would come to her senses. He didn't know what he'd do without her. He looked around at the spacious, clutter-free cottage. It was time to take a shower. Then he'd see how the little ones were doing.

A knock at the door made his breath catch. Maybe she wasn't still angry with him. He sniffed his armpit and grimaced. If she got a whiff of him, the last thing she'd want to do is cuddle.

"Hi, can I come in?" called Etienne.

"Hello, Mother! Yes, come on in. I'm done for the day. I was just getting ready to take a shower and head up to the palace."

She frowned. "I see," she said quietly.

He cocked his head. "Now what on Coldarius does that mean?"

She shrugged her shoulders. "What? I said two little words."

"It's not what you said, it's how you said it. Please don't tell me you don't like Princess Opal either."

"All right. I don't like her and I think you should stay away from her."

"Oh, come on, Mother! What has Legend been telling you?"

She sat on the settee and crossed her legs. "I don't need her to tell me anything about Princess Opal. I could school her on a few things. I've known her since she was a ChildForm, which means I know everything I need to and more. But what about you, my handsome son? How much do *you* know about her?"

He opened the small ice box to grab a cool drink for them. "She's the queen's sister. One day she was here, the next day she was on Earth. That's all I know." He opened it for her. "Come to think of it, I don't have any clear memories of her."

She accepted the drink. "I thank The One for that."

He groaned. "Don't you think you're being a little too harsh—"

"She's a killer."

He nearly dropped the cup. "What did you say?"

"You heard me the first time. She killed young Coldarians when she was a ChildForm. All because she didn't receive the attention she thought she deserved. I worked in the palace with Legend's parents. I was there for it all. She was pure evil, and I have no doubt she's still the same conniving, bloodthirsty little demon she was back then."

He stood rooted to the floor. His mother had just turned his world upside down.

"Those families never received justice for their losses. She got away with murder free and clear due to power and privilege. Once we discovered King Carlomon and Queen Elia had covered up what she'd done, we resigned from our positions and never spoke of it. Now she's back."

She drained the container in a single gulp. "More, please? Thank you."

His head was reeling from what he'd just learned. Quickly, he deposited the empty container, retrieved another one, and sat next to her.

She wrinkled her nose. "You smell of sweat and naivety. I want you to listen to me very carefully. The young MaleForm she murdered looked a lot like you. He wasn't a carbon copy, but close enough."

She pulled the thick, woolly hood from her head and set it aside. "I've seen the way she looks at you and I don't like it. She's spineless and self-deprecating—nothing like her sister. She doesn't know the meaning of honor nor does she show respect to anyone—not even her father. He loves her more than anything. I guess he has to—you can't choose your ChildForms."

She glanced at the family pictures on his mantel. "You're an AdultForm now. I can't stop you from living your life as you please. But I'll warn you, keep your distance from her. She's dangerous. If you reject her, she won't hesitate to hurt you."

He set the cup down. "She can't hurt me, Mother."

"Because of your condition?"

He laughed harshly. "If that's how you want to put it." Pivoting so he could look her squarely in the eyes, he said, "I can't be killed the way other Beings can. No weapon or poison can end me. When I first discovered I was...different...I thought you and Father already knew. But I quickly learned you didn't. For years, I've been afraid to tell you."

She touched his arm. "Why?"

He lowered his head. "I thought you'd cast me out from the family."

She set the empty carton down on the table with a sharp *plunk*. "Gallium! You're my son! How could you be so daft to think your father and I would abandon you?"

He turned his head to hide his tears. He'd been carrying the weight of his secret for too long. The endless fear of his parents turning their backs on him had all but driven him into despair.

She smacked him gently on the arm. "You have some nerve, young MaleForm! I've fed you. Clothed you and wiped your nose when you were ill. I've been the best MotherForm I could be, but you think I'm that shallow I'd turn my back on my own son? Neither I nor your father deserve that."

"I'm sorry, Mother," he whispered.

"You should be. If you weren't so stinky, I'd give you a hug. I accept you just as you are. Your gift...while I may not understand it...saved many lives on Platirius. When Sergeant Lionus described how you defeated the Kikhanians, no one was more proud of you than your father and I. And we always will be. Please get these silly notions out of your head. Have I been heard?"

A tiny smile peeked out. "Yes, Mother. You sound a little like Queen Dellah. Do you know why she killed them?"

"Arrogance. Insanity. Take your pick. She wanted the young MaleForm to love her. He didn't. He was already betrothed to another and they were in love. But none of that mattered to her. She's always believed she could take whatever she wanted because she was the daughter of a king. She doesn't respect boundaries. Now she's set her sights on you."

He twisted his lips. "I don't see that."

She pinched him. "That's because you're not opening those sparkling green eyes the WomenForms trip over themselves for. Her behavior at Queen Dellah's DeathCeremony was completely inappropriate. I saw the way she cooed and awed all over you in front of your fiancée. I have a lot of respect for Legend for holding onto her dignity. Had it been me, I would've punched her in the throat."

His head snapped up. "Mother!"

"I mean it. I would've knocked her out right there in front of everyone and awaited my punishment. She's callous and disrespectful. Please tell me you'll stay away from her."

He rubbed his eyes. "Mother, I made promises to Queen Dellah. Now, you've knocked me upside my head with this news, but nothing will stop me from being in the princesses' lives."

She side-eyed him. "I figured you'd say that. I understand where you're coming from, but Queen Dellah is gone. She has a father to watch over her daughters. We all loved her, but you're no longer under any obligation to her. You may not know this, but death severs ties between the living and those who ascend to the Afterlife."

She held up a hand to stop his next words. "You're young. You have to live your own life. I understand you love the ChildForms, but they don't belong to you. Whether you like it or not, King Dubian is their father. I doubt once he's released he's going to sit by and watch his daughters be reared on Coldarius."

She cupped his chin and turned his face to hers. "He won't, son. When he's ready, he'll come for the princesses. Then the battle over his daughters will be between him and King Carlomon. It's not your place to stop him."

"So what do I do? Just sit back and watch him steal them to raise them on that awful planet?"

"Gallium, have you heard a word I said? They're *not* your daughters. You have no say on who oversees their rearing. If King Dubian comes to Coldarius, I want you to stay out of it. It'll only make more trouble for you if you don't."

He sat back on the settee. She dramatically covered her nose. "Maybe you should shower. You don't want to scare the baby and make her cry. She has better lungs than most opera singers."

He laughed. "Mother, I don't know what I'd do without you."

She softly punched his arm. "Don't I know it? I can't imagine how my ChildForm's lives would be if I weren't around. I'm one of a kind, you know?"

His smile vanished. "Then promise me you'll stay with me for a long time. As in forever."

"I'll do my best." She sighed and looked around the neat, cozy cottage. "Our lifespans aren't promised, but I trust The One knows what He's doing. He's been good to me as far as I can remember. And He always will be."

She grabbed her bag and stood up. "Now that I've said what was on my mind, I'm going home. I heard what's been going on with you and Legend. I hope you can patch things up with her. Princess Opal isn't worth losing such an intelligent and beautiful partner. If you mess things up, you'll never find another like that one. Amos and I didn't rear you to be foolish."

He collected the containers and stood up. "I have no choice. It seems I'm going to have to protect her from danger too. If she's as crazy as you say she is—"

"She's right up there with the Amorous family."

"—then I'll keep my eyes on her. There was nothing we could do to stop her from coming back to Coldarius, but I'm not going to let her hurt Legend or the princesses."

She pulled the soft hood over her head. "And with that, I'm off." She kissed his cheek. "Ooh. You really smell."

"Gee, thanks, Mother."

"In a while, my stinky son."

"In a while, my beautiful mother."

Princess Opal is a murderer. I didn't see that one coming.

He stretched and headed for the bath chamber. He was looking forward to seeing the princesses again. As for their aunt, if she was looking to start trouble, she was in for a surprise. The biggest one of her life.

"See, Gallium? The baby bunnies are hopping around their mother!" said Princess Vivant.

Thanks to him, the palace gardens were beautiful this time of year. He filled his lungs with the fresh air, sighing with pleasure. He loved being back on Coldarius. Everything seemed cleaner and fresher at home.

He watched the tiny rabbit dart from under its mother and out again. Its siblings took turns sniffing each other and hopping about.

"Oh no!" she cried, pointing to the sky. A hawk swooped down and caught one of the babies in its claws while the other rabbits scurried away.

"He's going to kill the baby!" she sobbed. Suddenly, she picked up a rock and threw it at the hawk. It hit its mark and it dropped the rabbit. They ran to where it had landed. The hawk's claws had pierced its neck. It was struggling to breathe.

Impressed by her marksmanship, he said, "That was a good shot! Don't touch it, the mother may not want to care for it if your scent is on it."

She whirled around to face him. "But if we don't help it, it's going to die!"

He placed a gentle hand on her shoulder. "There's nothing we can do, Princess. It's already dying."

She glared at him defiantly. "No! I won't let it die!"

Before he could stop her, she bent down and picked up the animal. "You're going to get well and go back to your mother," she whispered to it.

From underneath her hands, an illuminated silver glow began to surround the bunny. He held still as a sweet scent filled his nostrils.

Smiling, she set it down on the grass. "See? All better? Now you can go back to your family." She pointed at the mother standing with her babies under a bush. "Go on. They're waiting for you."

He looked closely at the rabbit as it sniffed her hand before scurrying away toward its mother. Its wounds were gone! It hopped away just as healthy as it had been before the attack. Training his gaze on Princess Vivant, the hairs on the back of his neck stood up.

She watched the baby rabbit scamper back to his mother before turning to smile at him. "Did you see what I did? I made it well. That's the secret Mother told me I'm never to share with anyone except you. She said you would understand."

So she has a gift too—not like mine, but a remarkable gift. She has the power to restore life. "I'm very proud of you. You healed it."

She beamed at him. "Yes, I did. I don't like when things die, so I've decided I won't allow them to. I tried to save Mother, but she was too big. It only works on small things."

Her powers haven't matured yet. He remembered a time when he couldn't use the full benefit of his powers. *If only she could've saved her mother.*

Her eyes grew large with fear. "You won't tell my Grandfather or Aunt Opal, will you?"

"I'm not going to tell anyone. Your secret is safe with me."

She smiled up at him. "You're a good Being, Gallium. My father was wrong about you."

He ignored the urge to roll his eyes. "Oh? What did he say?"

Her silver eyes held a note of sincerity that belied her years. "He said you were far too arrogant for a commoner and you should be put to death. Slowly."

He shook his head. He wasn't surprised to hear what her father thought of him. "Well, everyone is entitled to their opinions, Princess."

"Gallium!" called Princess Opal. "You made it." She was carrying Princess Revari, who had seemed to grow overnight. She was able to hold her head up on her own and look around.

He accepted the baby and kissed her cheek. "Well, look who's here. Hello, Princess Revari. What have you been up to?"

The baby looked at him and cooed. "Oh? Learning how to run a kingdom already? That's a lot of responsibility, you know? I hope it won't tire you out."

Princess Opal laughed. "She's the best baby. She never cries and sleeps throughout the night. They're both so well-behaved."

She tugged on one of Princess Vivant's braids. "Are you hungry, cupcake? It's almost time for supper. How about you wash up and come down to the dining hall when you're done, okay? I requested one of your favorites, chicken pie!"

He looked at her suspiciously. Had she known chicken pie was one of his favorites too? He decided it didn't matter. If she was playing a game, it wouldn't work on him.

"Okay, Aunt Opal!" She kissed Princess Revari's foot and ran toward the palace.

She watched her until she was out of sight. "She's a delightful ChildForm. I wish my sister were here to watch them reach maturity."

He struggled to release his hair from Princess Revari's grasp. "You're a strong little thing, aren't you? Ouch! Can you let go please? I think you're a born warrior."

She focused her attention to the baby. "Yes, she has a strong spirit. I have a feeling she's going to be a fighter like her mother was. Not cowardly like me."

He kept his voice neutral. "I think you're being too hard on yourself. You're not a coward."

Her eyes took on a dark tone. "Dellah was the fighter, not me. She wasn't afraid of anything. Or anyone. She could make friends with anyone, while Beings just ignored me as if I didn't exist."

He noted the hard edge that crept into her tone.

Had she been jealous of her sister?

"But you," she said to Princess Revari, "won't allow anyone to push you around, will you? I know you won't."

Princess Revari gave her a toothless grin. "She's so beautiful," said Princess Opal. "I wonder, if I had ChildForms of my own, would they be this breathtaking?"

"I don't see why not," he said. "Is there someone you wanted to marry on Earth?"

She looked from the baby to him. "Me, marry a Human?" She chuckled mirthlessly. "I couldn't imagine lying with one of those filthy creatures. I'm a Coldarian and I belong with one. I'll find the one who's right for me right here at home."

"Well, stick to your convictions. I'm sure you'll find him in time."

He hadn't noticed the dull flatness in her eyes before. Queen Dellah's had sparkled whenever she was elated or angry, but it was difficult to discern Princess Opal's emotions.

"Shall we go in for supper?"

He hesitated. He wanted to find Legend and talk with her. She still hadn't taken his calls, and he was beyond exasperated with the entire situation. "I should get back."

She reached out and touched his arm. "But the princesses will be so disappointed if you leave now. You know how much they enjoy seeing you."

Princess Vivant stuck her head out of a high window. "Gallium, it's time to eat!"

"Well, I guess I've been summoned," he said.

She smiled at the now empty window. "I've found she's quite skilled at getting her way. I wonder where she gets it from?" she teased.

"Mm. Like mother, like daughter. All right, let us go. I could use a good meal."

She reached for his hand. He hesitated only for a second before he allowed her to grab it. He didn't want her to get the wrong impression, but after what he'd heard about her past, he didn't think it was wise to offend her.

Together, they walked hand in hand to the palace. If one didn't know better, they'd think they were lovers.

*W*hat did I marry? How could you stand by and allow them to take me and our daughter away!

King Dubian opened his eyes, still groggy from the sedative they'd given him to calm him down.

He'd lost track of how many days and nights he'd been in the Chamber of Despair. He'd hated every minute he spent there. The endless screaming and wailing were enough to make him end himself.

Get up and listen to me. Why have you allowed them to take me away?

"Dellah?" He sat up and positioned himself on the edge of the bed. He could barely lift his head.

Look at you. You can't even take care of yourself! Open your eyes and look at me. Look at me now!

He looked up to see her standing before him.

I want to come home. I belong on Platirius with you and our daughter.

"Yes. Yes, this is where you belong—this is your home. You know that."

But I'm not here, Dubian! You failed to protect us and now I have to make things right. I always have to because you're too weak to make a move without me!

"Please, My Queen. Please don't be angry with me," he begged.

Silence, you imbecile! You must go to Coldarius and bring me back. Then, everything will be as it should. Have I been heard?

"Yes, my love," he whimpered. "I'll do exactly as you say."

The figure vanished just as the door opened. It was King Micah. King Dubian adjusted his eyes to the light. *Who is standing behind him?*

"King Dubian," said King Micah. "General Kron and I have come to escort you back to the palace. You'll be released today."

His words felt thick and sluggish in his mouth. "General Kron? When did he become a general?"

"Today," he said. "I've defeated King Hitam and was appointed by my father. We didn't know when you'd be released."

He waved his hand. "I trust anything your father does. But I expect you to listen to anything Queen Dellah tells you to do. Don't try and go over her authority."

King Micah and General Kron shared a look. He read his father's expression.

Just go along with it for now, his eyes said.

"Uh...of course, King Dubian. I'd never try and overstep my place."

His black eyes narrowed. "See to it that you don't. My wife will have you executed for betraying her."

He nodded. "I understand. Let's get you back to the palace."

They assisted him to stand and supported him on both sides. His gait was slow and unsteady.

"What did you give him and how much did you administer?" asked King Micah. "He can barely walk."

The NurseForm looked nervously from King Dubian to King Micah. "We didn't have a choice, Your Highness. He was trying to hurt himself. Dr. Krause thought it would be best if he were heavily sedated."

King Dubian swiftly lifted his head. "Have her sent to the palace before dawn. I want to see her in my meeting chamber. Did you hear what I said, WomanForm?"

The NurseForm took a step away from his menacing gaze. "Yes, Your Majesty. I'll tell her."

His soulless eyes seared into her. "See to it that you do. Let us go."

Once they reached his bed chambers, he eased himself down on the spacious bed. "General Kron, we have important business to address. Make sure you're in my meeting chambers before daybreak."

"I will, King Dubian."

King Dubian looked at King Micah. "Are you staying?"

"No, I need to get back to Maieman. I came to...see how things were. Now that Lucian is back on Platirius and you're...in the palace again, there's nothing more for me to do."

"Please tell Queen Marietta that my wife and I look forward to seeing her soon."

He cleared his throat nervously. "Yes, of course. Lucian, I'm ready to leave now."

"Of course, Father. I'll escort you to your craft." He nodded to the half-dozen soldiers stationed outside the door. "If anything happens, come and find me," he ordered.

The soldiers saluted him. "Yes, General Kron!"

They didn't speak again until they were outside of the palace.

"He still believes his wife is alive," said King Micah. "He's too far gone to rule Platirius. What will you do?"

"I'll rebuild the army, just as we planned. Once the troops are dispatched here from Maieman and Platz, I'll have more than enough under me. He doesn't know anything about commanding an army. His strongest supporter is that old leader of the justice council. If I have to, I'll put him out of his misery. Don't worry, I'll handle him."

King Micah frowned at the palace. "You'll call if you need me?"

"You know I will. Give Mother my love, all right?"

They embraced before the king boarded the craft. General Kron waved until it was no longer in sight before heading back toward the palace, slowing his stride as it came into view. "You're not going to get in my way, King Dubian. By The One, I promise, you won't."

Quietly, Dr. Krause entered the palace. She was one of the few WomenForms that had remained after the

Coldarians left. She had been born on Platirius and wanted to die there. She had a bustling practice and hadn't seen the need to travel to Coldarius with the others.

She couldn't understand why King Micah had meddled in Platirius's affairs. Everyone was better off with King Dubian receiving treatment in the Chamber of Despair. He was just as ludicrous as before King Carlomon had him locked him up. Setting him free would bring nothing but chaos.

She sighed. She wished he'd stayed on Maieman, but it was too late now. She knocked softly on the door of King Dubian's meeting chamber.

"Enter," he said.

He was sitting across from General Kron at a short, round table. Her blood chilled when he looked up at her.

"No need to sit down, Dr. Krause, this won't take long. Seize her."

She let out a startled cry as two soldiers forcefully grabbed her arms. She looked at him for an explanation.

"You allowed my wife to be sent back to Coldarius. She told me she cannot return until you're dead." He stood up and addressed the soldiers. "Drag her out of here and set her down in the middle of the square. Then strip her and tie her down. I want all eyes to see her beaten for her incompetence."

She struggled to free herself. "And what incompetence would that be? You've been saying Queen Dellah is alive. How can you claim I'm incompetent if she's still alive? Both can't be true, King Dubian!"

General Kron looked away when King Dubian swiftly approached her and slapped her hard in the face.

"How dare you talk to me like that, you miserable excuse for a Being? You made my wife ill and helped her father steal her from me! Now he has my family! Did you really think I'd let you get away with it?"

Terrified by the lunacy shimmering in his eyes, she sought out General Kron. "Do you hear what he's saying?! He's gone mad! You know this! Why are you allowing him to do this?"

He ignored her while King Dubian slapped her again and yanked her by the hair. "One more sound out of you and your life ends right here. Take her away. Don't touch her until I arrive."

Powerless against the force of the soldiers, she whimpered as they violently carried her outside the palace gates. All the Platirians stopped and watched in confusion. She cried as they tore her clothing from her body and tied her wrists and ankles. One of them roughly pushed her to her knees. She shivered under the cool air.

Desperately, her eyes scanned the crowd, searching for anyone who would have mercy on her. The MaleForms looked at her with a sickening lust while a few of the WomenForms covered their mouths in horror.

No one knew what was about to happen. The WomenForms stepped back as King Dubian made his way down the palace stairs with General Kron and a group of soldiers in tow.

He looked down at her cowering on the cold, platinum ground. "You look like a trapped animal. It's fitting—that's precisely what you are. A filthy animal who has no business masquerading as a doctor. The only WomanForm with half a brain is my wife. How dare you try to steal her glory?"

He pointed a long finger in her face. "I know you tried to kill her! I intend to see you are properly punished!"

He turned away from her and sat down on a chair that had been brought from the palace. He nodded to a huge, muscular soldier standing a few inches from her. The soldier picked up a whip made from Antion.

Its handle was made of chrome, but the Antion whip was liquid fire. It cut through skin like a hot knife through butter. She screamed in terror. The WomenForms shuddered and stifled their cries. Surely he wasn't going to—

"Begin, and don't stop until I order you to," said King Dubian.

The soldier brought the whip down on her back. She wailed as the hot substance parted her skin. Without taking a breath, the soldier continued mercilessly beating her. Her terrified screams punctuated the sound of each lash. Blood splashed and pooled around her. The WomenForms choked on their tears.

The MaleForms, however, thoroughly enjoyed watching the disgusting act. The sight of her bloody, nude form and her screams enticed them. A few grinned at the horrified WomenForms.

After a while, only the sound of the whip buzzed through the air. Her silent form lay on the ground, cold and unmoving. King

Dubian raised his hand. The soldier checked for signs of life and shook his head.

"Bury her out in the Patachou field with the stray animals. I want her stench as far away from my palace as possible. And wash her filthy blood off the ground. I don't want my queen returning to see any of this."

He got up and turned to General Kron. "Well, Kron, shall we go have some luncheon? I've been informed the beef pie is particularly good today."

His gaze traveled from her lifeless corpse to the emptiness within the king's eyes. "I should stay and make sure they properly dispose of her. You go on, My King. I'd like to join you for supper if you don't mind."

He smiled, quite pleased with himself. "No, not at all. I look forward to it."

He started whistling as he turned his back on her corpse. He was still whistling when he breezed into the doors of the royal dining chamber.

General Kron glanced at her body before handing a heavy blanket to a soldier. "Cover her properly. Let's get her up to the hills." He surveyed the spectators. "The little show is over. I want everyone cleared out of here. Please don't make me say it twice."

Taking note that he led King Dubian's army, the crowd quickly dispersed. After witnessing the brutal attack on Dr. Krause, no one dared to challenge him.

"Bring the Dorgi around and place her inside. Gently," he ordered. A Dorgi was a small carriage used to transport large flower arrangements. The inside smelled sweetly of roses and the many other beautiful flowers it had carried.

The soldiers carefully picked her up and placed her inside. He pointed to the soldier who had beaten her to death.

"Since you did such a good job getting blood everywhere, I want you to clean these grounds until I can see my image reflected in them. Got that?"

The big soldier saluted him. "Yes, General Kron!"

He scowled. "Then get to it, you big beast. Let's go. I want to get her buried before the sun goes down."

They traveled until they reached the top of the hill. As they approached the Patachou fields, he kept going until he reached a beautiful field filled with flowers and greenery. Pointing to a particularly beautiful patch, he said, "Bury her over there. Once the ground settles, I want more flowers planted on the mound."

"Right away, General Kron!"

He thought of his mother as he watched the soldiers bury what was left of Dr. Krause. He had no intention of telling his father what King Dubian had done. Word would reach him soon enough, along with the rest of the galaxy. He finally understood why King Dubian was despised—he had no moral compass.

Demonstrating compassion was as unnatural to him as an eagle procreating with a bear. As the General of Platirius, he didn't want the reputation he was building to be tainted by the demented king's cruelty.

As Beings learned of the brutality behind Dr. Krause's death, he hoped they'd discover that he'd tried to restore her dignity. He hadn't wanted her to die—there had been no reason to kill her.

Yet he had been powerless to stop King Dubian. A WomanForm dying in childbirth wasn't unusual—Queen Dellah's death had simply been an unfortunate tragedy. He thought anyone of sound mind could understand that.

But the king was incapable of comprehending anything outside of his insanity. Being the leader of Platirius, General Kron was powerless to go against his orders. Especially with Chief Counselor Garoni watching his every move, just waiting to catch him in an act of treason.

Well, if he wanted to report where she'd been laid to rest, that was fine with him. He didn't fear any challenges. As unbalanced as he was, even he understood who was in full control of the military Platirius desperately needed.

If he decided to leave Platirius, all of the troops, with the exception of a few Platirian soldiers, would follow him. King Dubian was crazy, but not crazy enough to let that happen.

Without a skilled leader for his army, his enemies would swat him down like a fly. And he knew it. He doubted he'd hear any more about Dr. Krause after today.

When the hole had been dug deep enough, he went to the back of the Dorgi and removed a beautiful bolt of cloth made of gold and platinum threads. Under it was a large DeathCraft made of indestructible material. No water or dirt would seep through onto her.

"Wrap her carefully in this and transport her to the DeathCraft."

The soldiers quickly buried her while he recited a prayer his mother had taught him as a ChildForm. He hoped she'd entered The One's realm whole and at peace. When he finished, he scanned the beautiful field once again.

"Let's get back to the palace. The new troops should be arriving soon."

They quietly made their way down the hill, the soldiers' hearts swelling with pride at their general's sense of integrity. Although the Platirian soldiers would never admit it, they were relieved he'd returned from Kikhani. They hoped he would finally give King Dubian what he deserved. Only time would tell when or if that would happen.

Chapter 5

A soldier saluted King Dubian. "My King, there's a Coldarian WomanForm here to see you."

He looked up from the maps he'd been redrawing. "Who is it?"

"She says her name is Lady Alarah and she's married to General Iham."

He leaned back in his seat. "Send her in."

She strolled past the soldier, the sharp, spicy scent of her perfume lingering in the air. "Good morning, Your Highness. I heard you'd been released. It's good to see you back in control."

He raised an eyebrow. "I know who your husband is, but I don't believe we've met. Furthermore, there's not a single Coldarian left here. Why would you be concerned about me?"

"Because you made Queen Dellah so happy." The lie, as smooth as butter, hit its mark. Immediately, he straightened up in the chair.

Now I have your attention. "Not all of us wish ill will toward you, Your Majesty. Before you came into her life, I'd never seen her so happy. You're owed respect for all the joy you brought her."

"Well, thank you—Lady Alarah, is it? That's very gracious of you." He took in her fancy green hat with large feathers peeking out from behind. The dark green silk suit drew attention to her trim waist and large bust.

Her skin tone, much too bright for his liking, was set off by cold blue-green eyes, a regal nose, and thin lips. Clearly, she was attractive to many of the soldiers. They hadn't taken their eyes off her since she'd arrived. As for him, she wasn't as beautiful as his queen and never would be.

He gestured for her to sit down. "What can I do for you?"

"My King, I think it's simply tragic that King Carlomon split up your family with no thought of how it would make you feel. I can only imagine how much you miss them."

He set the pen down and reached for a small package. Opening it to inspect the contents, he removed a small, delicately carved razor. It was a gift from King Oni to congratulate him on his win against Kikhani. Onzi bordered between Platirius and Kikhani. He was glad it had remained one of their allies.

He opened it slowly, admiring the sharp blade and expert workmanship. Sliding a single finger over the blade, he looked into her eyes. "I don't see what that has to do with you."

She made a show of adjusting the elegant brooch pinned above her breast. She had become accustomed to drawing MaleForms in with her beauty. To her, he'd be no different. His eyes scanned her bosom before traveling to her face. She couldn't tell if she had enticed him or not.

"Unlike some of my neighbors, I respect you. You've brought a lot of prosperity to Coldarius—that shouldn't be overlooked. If I may, I'd like to help you reclaim your family so our planets may continue working with each other for mutual benefit. Queen Dellah worked hard to make the merger a success. Her contributions shouldn't die with her."

Die? What on Platirius is she babbling about? He shifted in his seat. "Go on."

"You can't get into Coldarius. There's a special shield that surrounds it so only we may pass. The Platirians that are on Coldarius got in because they followed us." She paused dramatically. "I can open the shield so you may collect Queen Dellah's vessel and your daughters."

Her eyes shifted to the blade in his hand. He'd been grasping it so tightly, ribbons of blood ran from his fingers down his wrist and spilled onto the maps. Not one to become queasy at the sight of blood, she maintained her cool composure.

Since insanity didn't scare her as much as poverty, she found it easy to overlook his strangeness—as long as she got what she wanted in the end.

"If you helped me infiltrate Coldarius, it would be treason against your king. Your husband is very loyal to him." He stared into her eyes. "Why aren't you?"

"King Carlomon and I have a long history. He may be the authority in Coldarius, but that doesn't mean I respect who he is and what he does. As for Iham...he's always been a disappointment. He's content to take orders while I've always dreamed of having more. My husband and I have very different values."

She opened her designer bag and took out a clean white scarf. Extending it to him, she said, "If we work together, we can both get what we want, Your Highness."

He reached for it and wrapped up his hand. "You still haven't told me what you want in return for helping me bring my family home."

She straightened her spine. "I want to be the next queen of Platirius."

He stiffened. She stood, walked around the desk, and kneeled in front of him. "May I?" she asked.

Not taking his eyes off of her, he nodded. Smiling, she secured the scarf around his hand. "The queen's death was unfortunate, but there's no reason to turn our backs on all the wealth we still have yet to claim. A kingdom's economy should always come before anything."

Still kneeling, she said, "I could be a valuable asset to you. You are a formidable king, but you need a strong queen by your side. Please accept my help? In return, I promise your happiness will be my first priority."

He was puzzled. Outside of his brief courtship of his wife, he had very little experience with WomenForms. Thanks to Queen Zherta's domineering ways, he'd always been too shy to communicate with them.

She reminded him of his stepmother—cold, calculating, and selfish. "What about the happiness of your husband?"

"What about it?" she asked frostily. Noting his bewildered expression, she said, "General Iham has tried to please me, but...he's failed. Over and over again. A good MaleForm should be able to please his wife in and out of the bed chamber, but I find Iham to be...very inadequate."

He raised his eyebrows. *My wife would never shame me this way.*

Not realizing disparaging another MaleForm's prowess hadn't scored any points with him, she continued with her deceptive ploy. "I've come to realize he'll never make me happy. I refuse to continue go on living unfulfilled. I realize my marriage was a mistake, but mistakes can be done over, yes?"

His head was swimming. The adulterous whore had no self-respect. "Please rise and return to your seat."

He'd allow her to believe she was using him. *After I bring Della home, I'll sit back and watch her deal with you.*

"All right, I'll take you up on your offer. Get us into Coldarius and I'll make sure you get what's coming to you."

She clapped her hands in delight. "Oh, thank you, King Dubian. You won't regret making me your next queen, I promise!"

His cold, onyx eyes assessed her. "I've always found regret comes far too late. By the time we realize the gravity of our actions, we're powerless to change the consequences."

"You're a very wise king," she purred.

"Thank you." He pushed a button on his desk. "General Kron, I need you in my meeting chamber."

He arrived in less than a minute. "Sit down, General. This is Lady Alarah. She says she'll help us get into Coldarius to retrieve my family."

Startled, he pivoted toward her.

Her blue-green eyes drank him in from head to foot. "You're a young one, aren't you? I never expected a ChildForm to beat the legendary King Hitam."

Offended by the slight, he met the king's eyes but kept quiet.

"The first rule as queen is to show proper respect to my general."

"Of course, Your Highness."

The tension in the room rose as General Kron observed the fashionably dressed female. He wondered what she'd said to King Dubian to set him off. More importantly, why hadn't she picked up on his dark mood? Or...maybe she had.

"I suppose you want us to eliminate your husband during this excursion?" King Dubian leaned forward, frowning at her. "Otherwise, you'd be a bigamist!"

For the first time, she withered under his scathing gaze. Collecting herself, she said, "I meant no disrespect to the Child—to General Kron. You already have a general. You wouldn't need Iham, and I doubt you'd want Gallium back on Platirius. Iham has had a good run, but his usefulness has worn out."

I knew she looked familiar! So she's General Iham's wife, thought General Kron. *And she wants him dead.* He hoped he'd never give his heart to such a treacherous WomanForm.

King Dubian peered at her over the desk. "And what of your daughter? Is she to be kept alive as well?"

Caught off guard at the mention of her daughter, her voice faltered. "Lyric is young. There's no reason to harm her," she said quickly.

He leaned forward. "Surely you don't think I'd bring another MaleForm's ChildForm into my palace to be reared along with my daughter?"

Doesn't he have two? She folded her hands. "I'd be willing to give up being Lyric's mother. I only ask that she be brought to Platirius to be raised with another family. She never has to know where she comes from."

King Dubian and General Kron stared at her in astonishment.

My wife would never abandon Princess Vivant. "Very well. Now let's get to what's important." The hate brimming in his sable eyes would've frightened someone more compassionate than her. "Tell me how to get into King Carlomon's palace."

Princess Vivant was sleeping when something awakened her. She sat straight up in bed and peered into the darkness.

"Hello?" she said tentatively. "Who's out there?"

Usually, the soldiers stationed outside her door would've stuck their heads in and assured her everything was all right, but no one came.

Throwing back the covers, she slid out of bed and into her slippers. Shivering, she wrapped the plush night robe around her and tied a firm knot. She hadn't taken a step before a hand reached out to her.

Before she could scream, a voice said, "Daughter. It's me. It's your father! Don't be frightened—I'm here to take you home."

Her heart was racing a mile a minute. She waved her hand to turn on the light and peered into his face. "Father!" she cried. "It is you!"

He placed a finger to his lips. "Shhh. I don't want anyone to hear us. Well, look at you," he gushed. "You've grown so tall! Yes, my little darling, I've come to bring you and your mother home."

She frowned. "What about my baby sister?"

A vacant look came into his eyes. "Your baby sister? What baby sister?"

She felt a chill go down her spine. Something was wrong. Why didn't he remember her sister? Maybe he wasn't better after all.

He placed a hand on her shoulder. "Can you take me to her? Please? I'd like to see her."

She nodded and took his large hand in hers. "Her nursery chamber is this way."

He held out a hand to stop her. "I know another way. I remember this room clearly. King Carlomon gave me a tour of the palace before I married my Dellah."

She shivered, but not from the cold. She'd never felt such dark and foreboding energy emanating from him before. She sensed his angry, confused thoughts rapidly racing together. "Okay."

104

He opened a secret wall that led them out of the bed chamber. Looking down at her, he whispered, "This path leads toward the east wing. Is that where she is?"

She nodded. "Follow me." She led him down the stuffy hall until they reached Princess Revari's nursery chamber. He reached up and pulled on a hidden knob. The door swung open, revealing a lavishly decorated chamber with hundreds of dolls and stuffed toys.

The tiny princess was sleeping peacefully in her bed. He knelt down and peered into her face. He took in the chubby cheeks and long eyelashes before placing a hand on her round belly. She was in good health. Suddenly, she woke up.

"Hi, baby Revari!" whispered Princess Vivant. She smiled at her sister and rolled over on her belly. Princess Vivant picked her up and kissed her.

"Baby Revari, we're going home to Platirius. Isn't that wonderful? Look? Father is here."

Cooing, she touched Princess Vivant's cheek before turning to look at him. Immediately, her eyes welled with tears and her lips trembled.

"What is she doing?" he whispered frantically. "Is she going to cry?"

She gave her a little bounce. "Oh, what's wrong, baby Revari? It's okay. He's not going to hurt us. He's our father."

His tone was flat. "She doesn't like me. Just hold her until we leave. I don't want her cries to awaken anyone."

"Are Grandfather Carlomon and Aunt Opal coming with us?"

"He's staying here—" He turned to look down at her. "Who is Aunt Opal?"

Once again, she felt the strange, ominous energy. She clearly remembered he'd spoken to her aunt before they left Platirius, but why didn't he? "She's mother's sister. She looks just like her."

Shadows of madness flowed through his mind. His eyes now glowing at her with interest, he kneeled down to her level. "Take me to her, please?"

When they reached Princess Opal's bed chamber, he placed a finger to his lips. "Stay here."

He crept slowly toward the bed. Looking down at her, he sucked in his breath. Lady Alarah had arranged for everyone in the palace to be drugged so no one would stop the Platirians from completing their mission.

Unaware of the danger standing before her, she slept soundly. He knelt before her and brushed a lock of her hair away from her face. *Dellah*. He scooped her up and lifted her from the bed. Securing her firmly in his arms, he carried her to the secret hallway where his daughters were waiting.

"Let us go." Quietly, he led them out of the palace to a carriage flanked by four soldiers.

"King Dubian," said a soldier. "We've secured the queen's DeathCraft in the back." He looked down at the sleeping WomanForm in his arms, then at the DeathCraft.

In the recesses of his warped mind, he believed The One had returned her to him in body and spirit. He rubbed his hand over the craft. *How fortunate.* He'd cherish the new, living vessel while carefully preserving the old one in his family's mausoleum.

Peering into Princess Opal's face, he said, "We're going home, my love."

He nodded to the soldiers and got inside the carriage. The soldiers lifted the princesses inside and shut the door. The night was eerily quiet as they left Coldarius. Princess Revari looked over her sister's shoulder at the palace, tears streaming silently down her cheeks.

The royal alarms sounded sharply against the cold winds. Coldarian soldiers rushed swiftly through the palace gates while King Carlomon threw anything he could grab.

"They've taken them! They've taken my daughter and granddaughters!" he roared. "Find Gallium and prepare to storm Platirius!"

"I'm already here, Your Highness."

He ran to him. "Gallium, they're gone. General Kron came last night and took them. The last thing I remember is all of us at dinner. Then, nothing! Do you feel a bit woozy?"

He shook his head. "No, My King. I feel fine."

"I sent General Iham to Earth on a temporary mission. Without King Dubian on the loose, I wasn't expecting Platirius to attack us. Please help me bring them back. I don't know what they're planning or why my family is involved."

Gallium poured a glass of water and handed it to him.

"They desecrated Dellah's resting place—what depraved mind does that? May The One help us if the Platirians have released him from the Chamber of Despair."

"How did they get past our security measures? I designed the shield so only those who share our DNA could pass."

"I have no idea. I gave my surveillance team strict orders to formulate it against them. I made sure they followed through. That means someone betrayed us. When I find out who it was, I'll execute them myself! Aiding and abetting the kidnapping of my family is treason!"

"Don't worry, we'll get them back. In the meantime, please stay here. There's no need for you to travel with us, Your Highness."

He sank into a high chair. "I'd be of more assistance if it wasn't for this blasted leg!"

Gallium stormed out of the palace and down to the gate.

"Coldarians!" he bellowed. "The Platirians have entered our home and stolen the princesses. I want every soldier at this gate, in full armor, ready to take Platirius now!"

The soldiers hurried to grab their weapons and don their war armor. Legend and two other WomenForm soldiers sprinted to the gate holding their weapons. The MaleForms stared at them in awe.

Looking her up and down, Gallium suppressed a spark of jealousy at the attention her curvy figure commanded. "Where do you think you're going?"

"I'm going to Platirius to retrieve the princesses!"

"Legend—"

She cut him off. "I understand you're a general now, but Queen Dellah trained WomenForms to fight when she was our general! King Carlomon has accepted us into his army! We have a right to join you!"

Etienne and Mrs. Guilde held each other's hands and looked on. If Gallium ordered the WomenForms not to go, they had to stand down. Legend looked up at the palace doors. Silence swept over the soldiers as King Carlomon stared out at them.

"I expect *every* soldier here to fight with honor. Please bring my daughters and granddaughters home."

Legend and the other female soldiers smiled at each other. They were going to Platirius!

Gallium stood in front of the troops and raised his weapon. "For Coldarius!" he thundered.

The Coldarians sounded a collective war cry. It was time.

G eneral Kron and his troops waited on the far side of a hill that intersected the border between Coldarius and Platirius.

"On my signal, you'll take out the target. Then we'll pick off the Coldarians like fleas." He spat on the deep purple ground.

Shortly before sunrise, his army had blocked off all the other entrances. Their enemies had one path to enter Platirius. He had no intention of letting them anywhere near King Dubian. Eliminating General Barrios was his top priority.

Legend walked behind Gallium. She hadn't seen him since they argued over Princess Opal nor had he said a word to her since they'd left Coldarius. She shook her head.

MaleForms and their stupid pride. Did he think she wasn't as good a fighter as he? She had no special abilities, but she was more skilled than some of the MaleForm soldiers in both armies.

A small stone rolled and landed a few feet ahead. Gallium abruptly halted and looked up into the hills.

Corporal Caswell looked at Corporal Snellings. "You stupid idiot! Keep still or they'll know something is up!"

Corporal Snellings ducked his head. "S–sorry! I had to scratch my crotch."

Corporal Caswell sucked his teeth in disgust. "Try bathing more. See if that helps." Sharing an assignment with him was giving him a throbbing headache.

Gallium continued surveying the rows of hills.

"What is it?" asked Legend. "What do you see?"

"It's not what I see, it's what I feel," he said. "The plants on those hills are carrying weight."

Puzzled, she adjusted her eyes on the numerous rows of hills. "They're carrying weight? What does that mean?"

"Shhhh," he told her. "Listen."

She stood still but couldn't hear a thing. Someone screamed in the distance. She looked up to see a Platirian soldier hurling toward them. A long vine was wrapped around his ankle. He screamed again as he was flung high into the air and slammed into a rock.

She watched as he was lifted and slammed into the rock in rapid succession. She looked at Gallium. His attention was fixed on the soldier. *It was him!* He was pummeling the soldier to death! The soldier's cries finally ceased. His motionless body lay sprawled before them.

He continued scanning the hills above them. "They're hiding in the rocks!" he shouted.

Masses of long, heavy climbers sprang forth and clutched the Platirian soldiers. They cried out in terror as they were flung high in the air and slammed on top of the sharp rocks.

"They've spotted us," shouted General Kron. "Take out Gallium now!"

Dozens of Platirians jumped out of the hills from the left and threw themselves on the Coldarians. From the right, a herd of them came for Gallium.

Legend lifted her sword and Azgoate. "Gallium!"

"Don't worry about me!" he told her. "Coldarians, kill them all!" he commanded. He clenched his fists and thousands of vines flew out of his chest, wrapping around the Platirians' necks. Sharp, snapping sounds of bones cracking could be heard over the commotion.

"Kill Gallium!" commanded General Kron. He sliced through a vine that encircled his wrist and ducked from another. "He can't concentrate on all of us!"

"You want to bet, General?" He flashed his hand out, and the huge boulder General Kron was hiding behind lifted into the air. Just in time, he jumped out of the way before it landed squarely down on him.

Legend and the other WomenForm soldiers fought their way through the Platirian soldiers, cutting off heads and firing on them. Brains slid out from the skulls of their enemies, making the ground slick with blood and brain matter. The Coldarians maneuvered carefully to avoid sliding on them.

Gallium gave the signal for the mounted soldiers to ride over the Platirians. They were crushed to death under the weight of the horses. Every soldier who came for him was killed.

He wielded thorny weeds from the ground, tightly coiling them around his enemies. They smothered some of them to death while slicing off the heads of others.

Finally, he found what he'd been searching for. The Aroshitz, a poisonous plant, was buried deep beneath the soil. He pulled it above ground, inhaled its venom, and blew it on the Platirian soldiers. Pieces of their skin melted from their bodies and fell to the ground.

General Kron swore. His ranks were depleting by the second. If he didn't stop Gallium, they'd all die. He crept closer to his target, then lunged out and grabbed Legend by the hair.

"This ends now!" he shouted. Gradually, the soldiers stopped fighting and focused on him holding a long blade to her neck. She struggled under his iron grip. "I eschew killing WomenForms, but I'll cut off her head unless you surrender!"

Gallium's fury rose. He advanced toward them.

"Don't listen to him," she panted. "Kill him, Gallium!"

General Kron smiled. "Who would've guessed you'd be the type to fall in love, huh? I don't like you, but I respect you, General Barrios. You're an impressive leader—I'll give you that. But I need you to surrender. If you do, I give you my word I won't hurt her."

He craned his neck to gaze at her face. "What a pretty WomanForm you are. Had you stayed home, you wouldn't be in this predicament. Why would you allow your WomenForm to fight? Do you see how weak she makes you?"

"He's more MaleForm than you'll ever be!" she hissed.

"Let her go, Kron," said Gallium softly.

"Oh, I will. As soon as you surrender to me."

"That's not going to happen! You stole the princesses!"

"I didn't. That was King Dubian. He infiltrated the palace and got them. Think about it. Do you think Princess Vivant would've followed me? She doesn't know who I am."

His fists clenched. "You're telling me he's walking around free?"

General Kron grinned at him. "Why not? He's the King of Platirius, isn't he? How long did you think he'd be locked up?"

"You're smarter than this, Kron. You know he doesn't care about anyone except himself! It was morbid to help him steal Queen Dellah's body! You should have more honor than that! He's going to destroy Platirius!"

"No. I'll be there to stop him. The throne of Platirius belongs to his daughters. I'm only helping to preserve it."

Gallium spat on the ground. "You don't give a damn about Queen Dellah's daughters. If you did, you would've let their mother remain resting."

"Oh, but I do! I respected Queen Dellah very much, but we all know you were the apple of her eye, weren't you? The ChildForms are where they belong—back on Platirius. I've been ordered to bring you in peacefully. I see how much you care about the princesses and this one."

He tilted his head toward Legend. "Spare her life and it all goes away."

He dropped the Azgoate.

"No, Gallium!" she screamed. "Don't listen to him! He's trying to set you up."

"That's it. Walk toward me and I'll release her." She struggled in his grasp, but he pulled her closer to him. "Be still if you don't want to see your lover get hurt. That's it. Just a couple more steps and we're done here."

114

Gallium had almost reached them when General Kron shouted, "Now!"

She screamed as a huge pendulum swung from the far side of the mountain and decapitated Gallium. The Coldarians shouted in disbelief.

She broke free of him and ran to Gallium, her arms outstretched. General Kron slowly approached and looked down at his body.

"King Dubian wants us to bring back his head," said a Platirian soldier.

He silently assessed the body for a few moments. "There's no honor in that. I don't need you to remind me what he wants. He doesn't command this army, I do. Collect the rest of the troops and let's get out of here. We've done what we came to do."

He saluted Gallium, then turned away, leaving Legend cradling him close to her chest, crying hysterically.

King Dubian pressed his face against a thirty-foot-high statue of Queen Dellah. He'd ordered for her DeathCraft to be locked away in the family mausoleum. A brazen sycophant, he was proud it was grander than the one King Carlomon had built for her.

"I brought you back just as I promised I would. Here is where your old vessel will stay while you and I rebuild what your father tried to destroy. We'll continue rearing our daughter to be a fine, upstanding WomanForm."

Soft whispers began growing louder in his mind. He turned to look at the window of his bed chamber. "Forgive me. I should've known you were so powerful you could return from the realm of The One."

The Platirians saw him whispering to himself and scurried away, terrified they'd draw his attention. "You can do anything you want, Dellah. You always have. I just have to make you remember me." He smiled—a vacant, most terrifying smile.

P rincess Opal awakened inside the bed chamber King Dubian had shared with Queen Dellah. Still groggy, she tried shaking her head to clear it. *What on Coldarius happened? Where am I?*

She tried to swing her legs over the bed, but it was difficult. "How did I return to Dellah's palace?" *The princesses! Have they been brought here with me?* She rubbed her temples. "Ohhhh, I feel terrible!"

The doors of the chamber slid open. King Dubian entered, an eerie smile playing around his lips.

By The One! she thought. *No!*

She noted his carefully crafted smile didn't match the sinister light in his eyes.

"You've been out for quite a while. Is there anything I could bring you? Soup? Tea? It's not yet supper time, but if you want, I'll have the dining staff prepare whatever you'd like."

She'd never seen eyes so black. They looked...soulless. "Where are the princesses?" she asked.

"Princess Vivant is having her nails done in her room."

"And Princess Revari?"

He paused for a moment. "Ah, yes, the InfantForm."

Her eyebrow rose. "The InfantForm? She has a name," she said dryly. "It's Princess Revari!"

"Yes, of course. Forgive me. It's going to take a while to get used to having such a small babe in the palace again. Princess Revari is in her nursery chamber. Would you like one of the NurseForms to bring her to you?"

"Yes," she said evenly. "And I want to see Princess Vivant too. How dare you take us from our home."

He sat on the bed next to her. She quickly scooted away from him. "This is their home. No ChildForms should be separated from their father—it's dishonorable."

"Where is the honor in stealing away three princesses in the middle of the night? My father must be going out of his mind!"

His smile was frozen in place. "It was your father who set this in motion. He had to know I couldn't live without my family."

"We won't stay here with you. Don't you see this is wrong?"

He shook his head and stared up at a life-sized painting of Queen Dellah. "The only wrong I see is the time I spent in the

Chamber of Despair while my daughter—daughters—had to go without seeing their father."

"A minute ago, you didn't even mention Princess Revari. Do you expect me to believe you actually missed her?"

"I would never lie to you. I'll cherish any part of you for the rest of my lifespan. As I said before...adjusting to the new baby will take some time. But I'm sure she and I will come to a meeting of the minds."

"Any part of me? A meeting of the minds?" she echoed. "She's my sister's baby, not mine. What do you wish her to do, sit down and discuss strategies with you like one of your soldiers?"

His laugh was hollow. "Your sense of humor is still infectious. You'll always be the most delightful creature I've ever met."

She unconsciously leaned toward him. "Do you realize I'm not my sister?"

The lustful leer he swept over her body sickened her. "You don't remember your old life, but you will. You've been under a tremendous amount of stress."

His eyes darkened until she could no longer see his pupils. "The trauma of birthing a second InfantForm has diminished your memory, but don't worry, my love. You'll be back to your old self in no time."

He's insane. There's no sense in trying to reason with him. He's convinced himself I'm Dellah.

"I don't know where you got those dreadful plain clothes, but I've dragged Marcia Blight back here to design a brand-new wardrobe for you now that you've lost the baby weight." He continued ogling her body. "Are you still the same cup size?"

Her silver eyes darkened to a cloudy gray. "That's none of your business," she snapped.

"Ah," he said. "Okay. Well, let me tell you what is my business. As we speak, my soldiers are getting rid of Coldarius's troops and the one they call Gallium. He's been a thorn in my side for years. I've ordered them to bring me his head so that I may look at it before I burn it."

She gasped. "And what of my father?"

"I haven't harmed King Carlomon. There'll be no need to go to war with Coldarius if he stays out of my way. I didn't want to be at odds with him, but he's left me no choice."

She altered her voice slightly. "How could you be so foolish?"

His smug smile vanished instantly. She tilted her head and narrowed her eyes in a perfect imitation of her sister. "Who told you to make a move on my home without my knowledge, Dubian? Didn't I warn you what would happen if you raised a hand to Gallium?"

He slowly rose from the bed, staring down at her as if he'd seen a ghost.

"Answer me, you weak cur! How dare you defy my orders!"

He sank to his knees. "Darling, you've finally returned to me. Please try and understand!"

Spurned by momentum, she hopped off the bed. "What I understand is, you've attacked my home. Do you realize, Dubian, without me, you'd be nothing? That Platirius would be nothing? If Gallium has been harmed, I'll have your head. That goes for your disrespectful general too!"

He held his hands up to her. "My Queen. I will make everything right. You'll see. Just give me a bit of time."

If only he knew how much she enjoyed making him dance like a puppet. "For your sake, I hope you do. Have my daughters brought to me. I don't want to see you again until I hear the Coldarian soldiers—especially Gallium—are safe."

Quickly, he got to his feet and fled the bed chamber. She stared at the closed door and chuckled. "Was that your plan all along, dear sister? To marry a weakling? He was so easy to fool!" She smiled to herself. "I hadn't planned on living here, but...this might be more fun than I imagined."

General Iham willed his horse to go faster while Dr. Barrios rode close behind him. They spied a crowd surrounding something on the ground. Legend was on her knees, wailing loudly.

General Iham jumped down from his horse and saw. *No!* He saw the head lying off to the side. She was holding his body in her arms.

"Gallium," he whispered. Every soldier bowed their heads.

Dr. Barrios came running over to them. "No! Gallium!" he cried.

"What will I tell Ezra and Etienne?" said General Iham. "And what of the princesses? King Dubian despises Princess Revari. Platirius is nowhere she should be."

As soon as he'd spoken, the winds began blowing harshly. Thousands of thistles, vines, and thorny plants began to sprout up from the hard earth. Gallium's body began to move on its own. Legend let out a startled cry when it broke free from her grasp.

She and the others watched in amazement as the body rose to full height. One hand stretched toward the severed head, willing it to rise until it connected with the body. Thousands of tiny veins sprouted throughout his body, filling with blood. Both arms raised toward the sky as Gallium became *whole* again!

"*Alabashee*!" he cried. The realm of The One opened and a hand reached down and pulled him up into the clouds.

"No!" Legend cried. General Iham held her back. "Let go of me! Where is it taking him?"

"Look, Legend," he said, pointing at the sky. "Look there!"

Gallium shot out of the sky, exploding into the ground at full speed. He tunneled deeper into the soil until he reached the axis of Space, then shot up out of the ground and back into the sky. There he was, suspended in the air. A cyclone of blinding colors surrounded him as numerous plants fused with his skin.

"*Basheelabey*!" he shouted. His deep, rumbling voice sounded foreign to them. They heard thousands of Beings speaking at once.

The skies opened wider as the voices chanted in a language they didn't comprehend. Believing they were witnessing an act of the supernatural, they threw themselves to the ground.

Slowly, he drifted down from the sky. The strange hues covering him merged into his body—his eyes changed from black to sea-green.

"On your feet, soldiers," he commanded gruffly.

Legend's head snapped up. "Gallium?" She got to her feet and ran toward him with her arms outstretched. "Gallium!"

He opened his arms and lifted her off her feet, breathing in her sweet scent. Tears of joy streamed down her face. She felt his heart pumping strong and fast against hers.

"You're alive! You're alive!" she cried. She cupped his face in her hands. "How is this possible? What were you yelling up there?"

A strange feeling rushed through her. It wasn't something she could explain, nor was she sure she wanted to. His energy channeled into her body, causing her to see flashes of images she couldn't understand. She looked into his eyes and all of a sudden, she *knew*. Gallium was a—

She fainted.

"Legend!" He shook her gently. "Come on, Baby, wake up! Legend!"

"Lie her on the ground," said Dr. Barrios. "She's fainted. The shock of seeing you—and all of this—was too much for her. I can revive her."

He placed a vial of Lorataz under her nose. Her eyes opened and she sat up coughing.

Gallium kneeled down and held her close to his chest. "It's alright. Just take a moment and breath."

The Coldarian soldiers were still bowing to him.

"Get up! I'm not higher than The One!"

Quickly, they rose to face him. Some, too afraid to look at him, averted their eyes.

"Gallium?" asked General Iham. "Is it really you?"

"It's me, General. Everything is alright now."

He turned to Dr. Barrios, who embraced him, slapping him hard on the back. Unlike the others, he didn't appear to be the slightest bit surprised by what he'd witnessed.

"It's good to see you back!"

"It's good to be back. No doubt Kron thought he had me. I can't wait to see the look on his face when he sees me again." He looked around at the Coldarians. "Were any of ours hurt?" he asked.

"Miraculously, the only casualties are the Platirians," said General Iham. "General Kron didn't bother to take the dead bodies back with him or give them a proper burial."

"What an ass," said Gallium. "They died for Platirius. The least he could've done is bury them."

A soldier pushed over a body with his foot. "Do you want us to, General Barrios?"

"No! They're not Coldarians! Leave them to rot! We have a mission to carry out." Thunder and lightning rumbled and crackled in the sky. "But it won't be tonight. Let's find some shelter and get supper started. We'll leave for Platirius before the sun is up."

"Do you think they've locked us out?" asked General Iham.

Gallium lifted Legend in his arms. "Our spies told me their shield is only closed to Kikhani. General Kron isn't sophisticated enough to calibrate it to deny access to multiple sets of DNA. Besides, the princesses have Coldarian and Platirian blood. No shield would keep us out anyway."

General Iham nodded. "Who in their right mind would let that monster out? King Dubian is far more dangerous than his father was."

Gallium looked over the horizon. "I don't know, but I'm more interested in finding out who let him in. When I find them...they're as good as dead."

Chapter 6

A few curious stares greeted Lady Alarah as she strolled around the palace. She didn't care. They needed to see who was next in line to lead by King Dubian's side. She hoped the Platirian soldiers had taken care of her husband. She wanted to focus on her future duties as queen, not worry about how to get him out of her hair.

The sun's rays illuminated tall, platinum candlesticks on an expensive buffet next to a stack of books covered in beautiful tapestry. If memory served her correctly, it had been in King Carlomon's study before Queen Dellah got married. She pursed her lips in distaste. She thought he'd taken all of her belongings with him.

She made a mental note to order the cleaning staff to remove the buffet and have it burned. She rounded the corner and headed toward King Dubian's bed chambers. She hoped to see him before he became immersed in the numerous responsibilities of running a kingdom.

Soft chatter and the babbling of an InfantForm caused her to pause at the door. Was he bonding with his daughters? She hoped not. There would be room for only one in his life after they married—her.

To someone with manners, entering his bed chamber would've been taboo. Since she believed she was better than others, rules simply didn't apply to her. She waved her hand over the TeleShield and gasped. Princess Opal looked up from changing Princess Revari's diaper and frowned.

"What on Coldarius are you doing here?"

She took a step forward, surveying the luxurious decorations and furnishings. "This isn't Coldarius, so one could ask you the same thing, Princess. Why are you in the king's bed chamber?"

She straightened up, tossed the soiled diaper into a bin, and picked up the baby. "Not that it's any of your business, but he brought us here. What's *your* excuse? Why are you in another MaleForm's personal quarters?"

She was puzzled, but would rather die than let the princess know. "I've come to speak with him. As the future queen of Platirius, it's only natural I'd want to see where I'll be sleeping."

Her cheeks puffed up. Lady Alarah snarled when she laughed in her face. Princess Opal looked at Princess Revari, who imitated her laughter. Together, they laughed until Lady Alarah reached inside the bin and threw the diaper at Princess Opal's feet.

"This will be my bed chamber. I won't have you creating messes and filling it with foul odors!"

Princess Opal stared at her in wonderment. "Wild pigs will sleep here before you. Had you bothered to change your own

InfantForm's diapers, you'd know the bin is specially designed to mask odors from diapers. It seems you've focused too much of your attention on being a whore instead of a proper mother."

Lady Alarah bristled. "How dare you speak to me like that!"

Princess Opal clucked her tongue. "You've always been high-strung, but this new wave of delusional thinking is a sign you're losing your mind. You're not royalty. I am. Did you forget never to show disrespect to a king's daughter? That's something you'll never be. You won't marry a king either."

She picked up her niece's diaper and returned it to the bin. "I don't know who placed these ridiculous notions in your head, but it's time to come back down to Platirius. Go home to your husband—while you can. Otherwise, you'll be punished for your insolence."

She stepped around her to place Princess Revari in the portable bed. Lady Alarah waited until she turned around, then slapped her across the face. Princess Opal returned the slap once. Then again.

"You filthy animal!" shouted Lady Alarah. "I always hated your sister, but even you have to admit you're a pathetic shell compared to her."

"What in Platirius is going on here?" shouted King Dubian.

The WomenForms turned to him.

"She struck me," said Princess Opal.

He ran over to examine her face. "Call for the chief royal physician!" he called to a soldier.

"We can't, King Dubian."

He whirled around to glare at the soldier. "Why?"

The soldier scratched his head. "Well, Dr. Barrios went back to Coldarius, and you had Dr. Krause killed. We have no chief royal physicians."

"Then find a trainee physician, you simpleton! Her face might be damaged!"

"Yes, Your Highness!"

He turned to face Princess Opal. "Are you all right? Does it hurt much?"

"It just stings a bit. I didn't expect her to hit me." She cast a suspicious glance at him. "Or to be here. Why *is* she here, Dubian? Is she the reason you entered Coldarius and took us?"

He licked his thin lips.

"Answer me. Did you conspire with her to attack Coldarius? Are you copulating with her?"

"By the Heavens, no, Dellah! I haven't touched her! I would never be disloyal to you!"

"Dellah?" echoed Lady Alarah. "She's no more Queen Dellah than I am! So that's it! She's deceived you into believing she's her sister. But the queen is dead! Everyone knows that!"

"You will shut your foul mouth this instant!" he snapped. "How dare you raise your hand to strike my wife!"

For the first time, the deranged look in his eyes terrified her. "But, I—"

"You shall be executed for striking a royal!" he roared.

Princess Revari, startled by the noise, began to cry.

"Dubian, you're scaring her!" admonished Princess Opal.

He looked helplessly from the baby to her. "Oh, I'm sorry, my Love."

"What kind of insanity is going on?" asked Lady Alarah. "You agreed you would make me queen if I helped you get into Coldarius! Now you're carrying on and acting as if Princess Opal is her sister? It's sheer madness!"

His inky, dark eyes cut into her like razors. "I never made any promises to you. Nor did you assist me. I entered Coldarius using a lock of my daughter's hair. You've only succeeded in proving you're a traitor to your planet and a self-seeking whore who's willing to throw anyone into the fire to get what you want."

She backed away as he advanced toward her. "Since you're so hell-bent on creating fires, I'll have one made especially for you."

She looked from Princess Opal to him. "What do you mean? What are you talking about?"

"Guards!" he thundered.

Five soldiers came rushing into the bed chamber.

"Yes, King Dubian?"

"Drag her down to the whipping post and strip her well. I want her beaten in front of all of Platirius. Then, drag her through the roads by her ankles. She'll be tossed into the Flames of Justice."

"No!" she screamed "You can't do this to me! I'm the wife of a general!"

King Dubian and Princess Opal laughed. "A general you wanted me to kill," he sneered. "I wonder if he'd save you if he knew what he married."

She cast a desperate look at Princess Opal. "He—he killed Gallium! I know you're in love with him! How can you stand by and let this happen?"

"The king has assured me no harm has come to Gallium." Princess Opal fastened a slim, platinum bracelet on her wrist. "Unfortunately, I can't say the same for you. You had the gall to come here uninvited and assault me."

She pivoted from the mirror to Lady Alarah. "You've never known your place—you were born as trash and you'll die as trash. It makes my stomach churn that you believed you were important enough to marry a king."

She turned to the soldiers. "You've been given orders. Take her away, but don't touch her until he and I arrive to see her punished. Have I been heard?"

They looked from her to him.

"Did you hear what my wife said?" he roared. "See to it!"

She screamed and tried to run as the soldiers seized her. A peal of delighted laughter interrupted her terrified cries. It was Princess Revari. She looked at Lady Alarah, laughing and clapping her small hands together.

Princess Opal smiled at her. "Are you enjoying the show, little one? Just wait. More is on the way."

Princess Revari's laughter was the last sound Lady Alarah heard just before they dragged her out of the palace.

L egend tried to stop staring at Gallium, but it was difficult. She, like the other Coldarians, was still trying to make sense of what she'd seen, but it was still too much to comprehend.

His blood had been spilled on the ground in front of her. Much of it was still splattered on her uniform. And yet, he walked by her side as if nothing had happened.

What had he seen when he journeyed into The One's realm? Had he always known he was different? Why had The One sent him back to them? So many questions flooded her mind, but she was afraid to voice any of them.

He looked at her out of the corner of his eye. He sensed her anxiety, but for the moment, there was nothing he could do to comfort her. He had indeed learned the secret behind his powers and...the meaning of his existence.

He felt more at peace than he ever had in his entire lifespan. He wanted to share all he knew with Legend...but it would never be.

There were rules within The One's realm—rules that must be followed. For now, it was enough that he'd returned to her.

He couldn't remember everything The One had shown him, but he knew grave danger was coming. He wished he could remember all the time he'd spent with The One.

For what seemed like minutes for the Coldarians was millions of years passing in a single moment. What did their futures hold? More importantly, would they have the strength to live through it?

She intertwined her hand in his. It felt warm and hard. He gave it a gentle squeeze, then let go.

"I have to keep my head in the game, Corporal Legend, or else I might lose it again," he said.

She sniffed and adjusted her hair. "That's a horrible joke," she said.

He frowned. "I wasn't joking. I want nothing more than to hold you, but when we're fighting, we need to keep it professional. General Kron knows you're my weakness now. I'm not going to let him get the upper hand over me again."

She nodded. "I understand, General Barrios. I promise I'll keep my hands to myself."

His smile didn't match the sadness in his beautiful eyes. "Thank you."

"Platirius is coming up," said General Iham. "Get ready. I think they expected us to turn around and run, but if I know General Kron, he'll have eyes on the gates."

"Good," said Gallium. "I'm ready for him too. Let us go!"

"Before we go, I think there's something we should address," said King Dubian.

Princess Opal laid a hand on a sleeping Princess Revari. "What is it?"

"I know you're my Dellah, but the others don't. Actually, it's none of their business. But now that you're back from the dead, I want everyone to know we're a united front again."

She unpinned her hair, letting it fall to her shoulders. "What are you going on about, Dubian?"

"Marry me again."

Her hands stopped in mid-air. "What?"

"I'm serious. The One interfered in our first union. Now that we're together again, we should make it official. Would you like to have a bigger wedding this time?"

If I married him, it would be easier to kill him and marry Gallium, she thought. "All right. I'll marry you...but I have a couple conditions."

"Just name them."

"First, we'll never share a bed chamber. Next, you have to ask my father's permission for my hand, and you must agree to expand Coldarius's borders so that it remains equal in power to Platirius. Otherwise, there'll be no marriage."

Bracing his arms on a chair, he pretended to mull over her terms. Confident they'd share a bed chamber in the future, he said, "I agree to all of it, so let's get it all taken care of. Please call him on the TeleScreen."

She scanned her hand across the TeleScreen. "Hello, Father. I hope you haven't been too worried. We're all right."

King Carlomon quickly set his drink down. "By the Heavens! I'm so glad to see you. How has that brute been treating you?"

She turned to King Dubian before turning back to her father. "Quite well, actually. I learned how the Platirians broke into Coldarius. It was Lady Alarah who gave them access."

"What? Her? Why would she betray us?"

She smiled. "Apparently, she thought she would be the next Queen of Platirius."

He set his cane aside. "That's ridiculous! She's already married! I honestly don't know what to say to General Iham, but I'll have her head for her treachery! I warned her not to cross me."

"We're taking care of her here."

He moved closer to the TeleScreen. "What do you mean, 'we'?"

She sighed. "Father, he's asked me to marry him—"

"No! I won't allow it!"

"You didn't let me finish," she said evenly.

"I'll agree to it if you give permission and if he agrees to continue expanding Coldarius's borders. You know as well as I do, we're not able to do it on our own."

She sat back and crossed her legs. "Without Platirius's resources, it would take years before we reached the level it's on now. The foundation has already been laid. We'd be foolish to watch it all go to waste."

"Opal, listen to me. There are far more important things than wealth and power."

"Not to me," she said quickly. "This is what's best for Coldarius. You were in agreement before, so I see no reason to throw everything away now. In your heart, you know I'm right."

"But he—"

"Is fully on board with any decisions I plan to make," she said coolly. "Please don't fight me on this. We need each other to survive."

He rubbed his hands over his eyes. "Where is Dellah's—"

"Properly stored in a beautiful mausoleum," she interrupted. "I plan to brief you on everything once I come to visit. Please grant us your blessing, Father."

He would have rather resurrected King Anemi than give King Dubian permission to marry his only surviving daughter. Yet, he knew he had no choice. If she was determined to marry him, nothing he could say would change her mind.

King Dubian may not know what you're thinking, but I do. You want to murder him and replace him with Gallium. "All right. I'll have a contract drafted within a half-hour span. Once he signs everything, you may move forward with the marriage."

"Don't worry about the contract. I've already had one drafted. I copied and pasted all the stipulations from the first merger."

He stood still. "You have? When?"

"The first morning I woke up on Platirius," she said smugly. "I felt it would come to this, so I wanted to be prepared. Dubian will sign it before we marry. I thank you for your support, Father. You don't know how much this means to me."

She ended the call and turned to King Dubian. "Let us sit down and settle the contract. I don't want to keep Lady Alarah waiting."

After he scanned his signature to her palm, he said, "How long will it take you to plan our wedding? Do you want it to be grander than it was before?"

She pinned up her hair and straightened the form-hugging, plain black dress. She stood admiring her reflection in the mirror. "I don't want it to be grand at all. And I know the perfect place and time."

He smiled at her. "Where and when?"

Returning his smile, she said, "Here. I'd like to get married in front of the Flames of Justice right before we toss Lady Alarah into them."

His smile vanished. He stared at her as if he'd never seen her before.

She cocked her head. "Is something wrong?"

"You...want us to take our nuptials in front of the Flames of Justice? There are Beings who have suffered for thousands of years in the flames. Won't that ruin the moment for you?"

She shook her head. "Not at all. I'd love to hear them screaming while I promise to honor you." She turned to the mirror and applied a fresh coat of lipstick. It was almost as black as his eyes. "Nothing would make me happier."

A chill spread through him, but he said, "As you wish, dear."

Princess Opal watched the blood splatter on Lady Alarah's naked back. She silently admired the brutality of the large, muscular soldier who wielded the Antion whip with such a force, it tore chunks of flesh from her body. Her screams could be heard throughout the courtyard. The Platirians watched as he viciously beat her.

Gallium and General Iham entered the palace's gates and stationed their soldiers in inconspicuous areas to avoid detection.

"That sounds like my wife!" cried General Iham.

Gallium grabbed his arm. "If it is, you can't go charging in there. And what would she be doing on Platirius anyway?"

King Dubian's voice boomed over the crowd. "Now you'll tell everyone of your wicked deeds. What have you done to deserve this?"

She lay with her face buried in the ground, sobbing aloud.

"Speak, you treacherous WomanForm!" he shouted. "Let everyone here know what will happen if they forget their place!"

"I struck Princess Opal! And I–I betrayed Coldarius. I let the Platirians in to steal Queen Dellah's daughters," she cried.

"And? What else have you done? Let everyone hear how abominable you are."

"I—I planned to have my husband executed. I wanted him dead so that I would become the Queen of Platirius."

Feeling the blood run down her face from the gashes on her head, she panicked. *Has my face been ruined?*

"And...my daughter... I sold her to a Platirian family on the promise I'd never tell her I was her mother. I betrayed my family and my planet!"

She began sobbing again. One of the Platirians spit on her. Then another, until all of them spat on her. The soldier raised his hand to strike her again, but King Dubian held up his hand.

Gallium placed a hand on General Iham's bowed head. "I'm so sorry. I had no idea it was your wife who betrayed us."

"How could you know?" he said sadly. "How could anyone have known what she was capable of? Our daughter is all we have. She sold her, Gallium." His voice broke. "She sold her as if she were nothing more than a bauble."

"They're going to kill her, but not out of respect for Coldarius. This is an example of King Dubian's madness. He's enjoys watching females suffer. Do you want to try and save her?"

General Iham's eyes were hard. "She's earned her fate. Let them do what they need to do with her. My focus is finding my daughter and taking her home with me."

Gallium nodded and looked through the binoculars again. "That's Princess Opal standing next to King Dubian, but I don't see Princess Vivant or Princess Revari. What is she doing?"

Dr. Barrios crept up behind them. "General Kron and the others are in the medical chamber receiving treatment. If you strike fast, you can take them by surprise."

"Wait a minute," said Gallium. "What are they doing now?"

The soldiers had gathered up Lady Alarah. Everyone followed King Dubian and Princess Opal to the other side of the palace.

Gallium put away the binoculars. "Let's move along the outer wall and follow them."

They traveled across Queen Dellah's well-manicured lawns to a mysterious field of high flames in beautiful colors swirling together.

"We're behind the justice chamber," whispered Gallium. "Those must be the Flames of Justice."

The immortal flames swirled in dazzling shades of platinum, lavender, and blue. They saw figures moving around in the flames, but didn't recognize anyone nor could they decipher what they were doing. Although the flames looked magnificent, the screams emanating from them suggested the captives wished they were free of them.

"I've never seen them up close before." said General Iham.

"The flames never extinguish," whispered Gallium. "Whoever gets thrown into them spends an eternity burning. Their souls never ascend to the Heavens."

Dr. Barrios adjusted his glasses on his nose. "By The One, are they going to throw her into them?"

Gallium nodded. "It looks like they are."

"But I thought the flames were reserved for Beings who had trials. She betrayed Coldarius, but who has she harmed on Platirius?"

"We're about to find out," said Gallium.

The soldiers forced Lady Alarah to kneel before Chief Counselor Garoni. He loomed over her, dressed in robes just as dark as his eyes. Scowling down at her, he said, "Lady Alarah of Coldarius, you have been found guilty of striking a royal figure. Kneel and await your punishment."

He turned to King Dubian and Princess Opal. "King Dubian, do you take Princess Opal to be your queen?"

"I do," said King Dubian.

"They're getting married? What on Coldarius is going on? And who did Lady Alarah hit?" whispered Dr. Barrios.

Gallium was just as bewildered. "Shh. They'll hear us."

"Do you, Princess Opal of Coldarius, take King Dubian as your husband?"

"I do," said Princess Opal.

The Chief Counselor bristled under thick, black eyebrows. "Then, by the power bestowed to us by The One, the greatest power in all of the galaxy, I now pronounce you the King and Queen of Platirius."

No one clapped or cheered as King Dubian turned to Princess Opal. She gave him a quick, chaste peck on the cheek.

"Gallium," said General Iham. "I don't think we'll be taking the princesses back with us to Coldarius. I've just received a transmission from King Carlomon. He's given his blessing to this nightmare."

Gallium stared at King Dubian and Queen Opal in disbelief. "I think you're right, General."

They heard Lady Alarah scream as she was tossed into the Flames of Justice. Through blurred vision, General Iham watched her inspect her surroundings before waving her hands in front of her face, trying to ward off the scorching fire.

He could see no physical changes to her skin, yet her agonizing screams told a different tale. Out of respect, Gallium and Dr. Barrios stood quietly, waiting for him to compose himself. He continued watching the flames torment his wife while King Dubian and Queen Opal openly jeered at her.

With eyes colder than a winter's night, he said, "Let's head home."

M aking the transition from Coldarius to Platirius was easy for Queen Opal. She followed her sister's example and brought many Coldarian soldiers back to Platirius with her—including General Iham.

King Carlomon told her he would rest easier knowing some of his best would be around to protect her, but Gallium chose to stay behind.

She had hoped her marriage would make him jealous. It didn't. He understood why her sister married King Dubian—for the advancement of Coldarius. But Queen Opal married him for her own personal ambition. He saw no reason to risk his life for such selfishness.

To his surprise, King Carlomon hadn't asked him to go to Platirius. He was grateful for that. Although he missed the princesses dearly, he couldn't stomach being so close to their father again.

General Kron had been shocked and outraged once he learned Gallium had survived the attack. He didn't care. As long as he didn't try to enter Coldarius again, the king's general would keep his life.

A few years passed before he'd see the princesses again. The time on Platirius and Coldarius was different from time spent on Earth. Once Coldarians reached a certain age, their youth remained. He looked no different than he did when Queen Dellah passed.

As for Princess Vivant, she was blossoming into a breathtaking WomanForm, while Princess Revari was seldom seen. Rumors swirled that her father treated her abhorrently when she was out of Queen Opal's sight.

Had she learned of his sneaky ways, she would've retaliated against him. Her heart was just as dark and evil as his, but she genuinely loved her nieces. He knew better than to let her discover his contempt for his youngest daughter.

She sent another message that she wanted to see Gallium. He disconnected the transmission. He had nothing to say to her. It was the night of King Dubian's thirty-ninth LifeCelebration. He'd invited the kings from all the realms to join him, but King Carlomon had declined to go.

Although Queen Opal and he were married, King Carlomon still hated him for stealing Queen Dellah's DeathCraft and his family. King Dubian's twisted mind had finally reconciled she was not his former wife, but as long as he could pretend she was still alive, it didn't bother him.

She still refused to share his bed. Unlike her sister, she was extremely shallow. She wasn't attracted to her husband—it was Gallium she wanted. For years, she plotted how she'd betray him and make Gallium her king. The first leg of her plan succeeded when she'd enticed Legend with a position in Platirius's army.

With her and Gallium living on different planets, she hoped the distance and Legend's ambitious nature would place a strain on their relationship. It was working.

The lovers saw very little of each other. He was beginning to believe they'd never be together. But Queen Opal had one more trick up her sleeve to get Legend out of her way.

She summoned her to the palace just before the LifeCelebration began. "I'm glad you could come on such short notice, Legend."

She bowed to her. "Hello, Queen Opal. I hope I didn't keep you waiting long." She wondered what she wanted with her. It was no secret the queen was a snake—shrewd, selfish, and condescending.

Although she fulfilled Queen Dellah's wishes in recruiting WomenForms into Platirius's army, she'd done nothing to protect them from the constant harassment from the MaleForm soldiers—especially her.

She ordered all of the Platirian WomenForms who had traveled to Coldarius to return to Platirius with the promise things would be better. They quickly learned she had no interest in protecting their rights. She was content to stay in the shadows while King Dubian and General Kron controlled everything.

"Legend," she said sweetly. "The king doesn't believe in sending WomenForms to Earth for missions, but I do. I'd like to send you to Earth for an extraordinary project. You'd travel to the year 1956, in a place called North Vietnam. Your mission is to observe the Humans until the war ends."

She uploaded photos on the TranScreen. "Of course, King Dubian wouldn't know anything about this. You'd report only to me. Our Platirian shield would hide you from the Humans, so you could fight and kill as many Human soldiers as you'd like without detection."

Queen Opal stared at the TranScreen, enthralled by the bloody images. "This is an experience of a lifetime. You'd gain skills and knowledge you wouldn't acquire here."

She disconnected the signal. "I'm aware of General Kron's discriminatory views against WomenForms. He doesn't want them in his army. But now that I'm queen, I didn't give him a choice. I believe if WomenForms want to risk their lives for their planet, they should be allowed to."

She cupped her chin in her hands. "You'd return to Platirius as a fierce fighter. Even better, the experience would put you in line to be the first WomanForm general on Platirius. I know that's what you've always wanted. What do you say? Would you like to take some time and think it over?"

Legend expelled a breath. She couldn't argue with anything she'd stated. Things were hard for female soldiers due to General Kron and King Dubian's misogynistic views.

She doubted she'd ever be appointed to general as long as they were in control. On the other hand, if she went to Earth, it would be a long time before she'd see her mother and Gallium again.

Gallium. The distance had already driven a wedge between them. Would this be the last straw for him? She wouldn't know until she spoke with him. She had to see him—tonight. If he wouldn't support her goals, she'd rather know now than later.

"Yes, but I'd like to return home for a couple days. Then I'll have an answer. Would that be all right?"

Queen Opal smiled at her. "That's perfect. Take all the time you need. If you don't want to go, I'll understand. The mission isn't mandatory. I'll just send another WomanForm in your place."

Legend bowed to her. "Thank you, Your Majesty. I won't keep you waiting."

She doubted the queen was sending her to Earth for her best interests. Where Queen Dellah was open and straightforward, her sister always had an ace up her sleeve. She and King Dubian were perfect for each other—evil and overly self-absorbed.

Even Princess Vivant, who had grown to be a lovely WomanForm on the surface, had grown to be dismissive and haughty under their tutelage. She hoped Princess Revari would continue to be the happy, bubbly ChildForm she'd always been, but she wasn't so sure.

She'd found the young princess crying after King Dubian had informed her he wouldn't hold LifeCelebrations for her as an excuse for killing her mother. After having a revealing conversation with her mother about her birth father, Legend already despised him.

Although Queen Opal took the reins in ensuring Princess Revari had LifeCelebrations, the callous way the king treated his youngest daughter made Legend wish he was dead. She was growing up fast. Too fast. Her young mind was attentive to everything in her external environment.

She would need someone other than her aunt to protect her if she left for Earth. Her husband was a poser—he knew how to maneuver around her to hurt his daughter. It would be a tragedy if she grew up to emulate either of them.

She could count on Gallium to help shield her from his pettiness and cruelty. She knew he wouldn't attend the LifeCelebration. Tonight would be the perfect time to talk to him. She only hoped he'd be willing to stand by her.

B reathing harshly, General Kron leaned against the door of King Dubian's meeting chamber. He couldn't believe what he'd just heard. He wanted to warn the Coldarians of the king's plans, but doing so would be treason.

His head swam not just from the strong drink he'd consumed. King Dubian had spoken of murdering billions of innocent LifeForms as easily as he discussed the weather. Blood. There would be a river of blood on his hands and there was nothing he could do about it.

He thought of his parents. Would they still be proud of him once they learned he'd helped him exact his revenge on the Coldarians? And what of Princess Vivant? What would she think? No. She could never find out.

Their friendship had rapidly blossomed into something he hadn't realized existed. No matter what he had to do, she could never know he had a hand in something so dastardly. He silently prayed to The One for forgiveness. Even if it were possible, how would he ever forgive himself?

Chapter 7

Gallium's eyes were cold. "So you're just going to go to some foreign planet for who knows how long on the promise that she'll make you a general? After years of being hell-bent on convincing me she hates you, now you're suggesting she's looking out for your future? What about us, Legend? I asked you to marry me years ago. How long am I supposed to wait?"

She folded her arms. "I never said she's acting in my best interest, but this is an opportunity of a lifetime. You knew from the beginning my career was important to me. Don't act as if you haven't. It's okay for you to go and fight whenever King Carlomon wants, but I'm supposed to sit at home and raise babies?"

He held onto what was left of his patience. "I never asked you to do that. I'm not even sure I'm able to have ChildForms, but if I can, why shouldn't I have the chance to be a father? And yes, they'd need a mother to care for them. Not some WomanForm walking around constantly waving her weapons in the air. I don't know what you're trying to prove!"

"I'm not trying to prove anything to anyone!" she shouted. "Why can't you understand this is what I have to do?"

He closed the distance between them. "What I understand is, I don't matter to you. I'm something like this potted plant here."

He tapped a jardiniere. "Something for you to wet with your lips and talk to occasionally before you run off to do more important things. You don't want me, but you don't want anyone else to have me. Isn't that right?"

She pushed him away. "Anyone else like who? Queen Opal?"

"Oh, don't start. She's married to King Dubian now. I'm sick of hearing that tired old excuse. Don't bring her into this. This is about you and I."

"I know she married him for power," she countered. "Everyone knows that. According to the gossip, they don't share a bed. Do you know what that means? She's keeping her side of the bed warm. For you."

"Well, at least I'd be keeping someone warm, eh?"

His condescending tone enraged her. "Well, why don't you? Why don't you just slit King Dubian's throat for her and make all her dreams finally come true? It's not as if she can kill you like she killed those other Coldarians. You don't die, remember?"

Her words tore into his soul. He never thought she'd use his abilities against him. He had hoped she'd accept him for who he was.

"You want to know what dies when you throw my condition in my face? My heart. You rip out pieces of it every time you say things like that. I can't help the way I was born!"

She reached out to him, but he pulled away. "No, don't try to clean it up now! I know I'm not like everyone else! I have to live with it every day—isn't that enough? Maybe that's what it's been all along. You could never love an abomination like me. You just didn't have the heart to tell me until tonight."

Tears sprang in her eyes. "That's not true! I would never think of you that way!"

He turned his back on her. "Just go. Go to Earth if it makes you happy and gets you one step closer to becoming a prized general. I realize now I'll never make you as happy as you are when you kill. For me, it's a job, but I think you enjoy it. You complain how Queen Opal lacks compassion, but in some way, I think you're more ruthless than she is."

She refused to allow the tears to fall but couldn't help her lips from trembling. "Well, I guess I have my answer, don't I?"

"I guess you do," he said. "You knew what I'd say before you came here. We're over. After tonight, you'll never have to worry about me again."

He stormed toward the door and slammed it.

"Damn," she said.

She ran to the window and watched his tall frame disappear into the night. She allowed herself to cry for everything she'd lost and everything she'd gain. He was gone. She'd hurt his pride for the last time. He was never coming back. Now, she had to look to her future. A future that didn't involve the love of her life.

Queen Opal brightened when she saw Legend coming down the hall. "Legend! I didn't expect to see you so soon. I'm on my way to the dining chamber for breakfast. Have you eaten?"

She bowed to her. "Good morning, Queen Opal. No, I'm not hungry. I just came to tell you I'd like to go to Earth."

Her silver eyes flashed with triumph. "That's wonderful to hear. I'll make the arrangements to send you off right after breakfast. Have you said goodbye to everyone you needed to?"

Legend didn't miss the false concern in her tone. She was determined not to show how heartbroken she was in front of her. She straightened her shoulders and put a false brightness in her tone. "Yes, I have. Everything has been taken care of." If she found out she and Gallium had broken up, it wouldn't come from her.

"Excellent! I'm so glad you're doing this for us. Platirius will thrive from the knowledge you'll acquire." She gave her arm a gentle squeeze. "Thank you so much."

Briskly stepping around her, she headed toward the dining chamber. Legend never saw the evil smirk on her face.

A few hours later, Legend was on a craft headed for Earth. As Platirius grew smaller, Coldarius came into view. Her eyes filled with tears. Everyone she loved was there. She missed them already.

"Gallium, if you swing that ax like that again, I'm out of here. I didn't return home to let you kill me!"

He brought the ax down on the wood again.

Dr. Barrios looked around in amazement. "You have enough wood here to keep us warm for years. How much more will you chop?"

"Leave me alone, Barrios. I'm in no mood."

He eyed him suspiciously. "I can see that. Did you and Legend have a disagreement?"

"Yes." The sound of the ax punctuated his words. "And I don't *chop* want *chop* to *chop* talk about it!"

He wished there was something he could do to help him, but he knew his brother's moods. "I'm sorry. I hope you'll be able to work it out. I know how much she means to you."

Gallium kept his eyes on the task.

"Well, if you need me, I'll be around."

He continued swinging the ax as he walked away. He promised himself he'd never allow another female to hurt him. Legend had ripped his heart out, turned on her high-heeled boots, and never looked back. He wanted to wish her well, but couldn't.

At the moment, he hated everyone and everything. He hoped in time his heart would soften, but forgiveness wasn't in his immediate plans. The sound of the ax whirled through the air as it continued to hit its mark.

"Is it ready?"

"Yes, King Dubian," said a dining staff. She handed him a beautiful crystal bottle.

He took it without a word. He didn't believe in thanking commoners. He was on his way to Coldarius—a trip he hoped would be successful.

King Carlomon opened the door. "King Dubian? This is a surprise. I've given my staff the day off. What brings you here?"

"Yes, I remember when I used to come here with Queen Dellah. Today is some sort of celebration for the commoners, right? I haven't forgotten my time spent here with her. I hoped we'd have good times like that again, but since I married Opal, you've kept your distance."

He lifted the bottle of ChayBerry wine. "I'm hoping to change all of that. You were a wonderful father figure to me. I'd like to win back your respect."

Reluctantly, he let him in. He wanted nothing to do with him, but he heard Queen Elia's voice. *Blessed are the peacemakers...*

Leading him into his spacious private dining chamber, he retrieved two glasses and set them down on the table. He added a round of cheese and an assortment of crisp, buttery crackers to a polished circular board and sat it next to the glasses.

Filling a glass with the fragrant wine, King Dubian smiled.

"Aren't you having some?" asked King Carlomon.

"No, I drove myself here. I didn't want to take advantage of your generosity and ask to stay the night. I never could handle spirits anyway. But if you don't mind," he said, looking at the oversized ice box, "I'd love some sweet PotterBerry juice, if you have some?"

He nodded. He got up to retrieve the juice and poured a large glass for him. "I hear you've transferred many of my wife's relatives to Platirius."

He smiled. "Yes, well, Opal was lonely. I figured it would make her happier to have her extended family with her. All that's missing is you."

Once he drained the glass, King Dubian quickly refilled it. "I have no desire to live on Platirius. This is my kingdom and my home. I'm sure you understand, I have Beings to care for."

King Dubian kept up a lively conversation until he saw the last rays of the sun begin to fade into night.

King Carlomon nodded as if he were falling asleep. "By the Heavens, I don't know what's wrong with me. I feel so drained."

King Dubian's smile faded. "You should've eaten some of the cheese. It would've been less painful for you."

King Carlomon looked at him sharply. "What?"

"At least you have proper table manners. My father was a glutton. He could drink a whole flask of wine in one sitting. That made it much easier to put him out of his misery."

A chill went down King Carlomon's spine. "What are you talking about?"

King Dubian ran a lone finger down the neck of the bottle. "Were you aware I killed my father? Surely you've heard the rumors. When I was younger, I learned there are several ways to kill a king and claim his planet."

He eyed him surreptitiously. "Taking his head is the quickest way, but that's the old way. It's boring—not enough imagination goes into it. Sometimes," he said, reaching for King Carlomon's wrist, "you only need a bit of blood."

"What on Coldarius are you doing?" exclaimed King Carlomon. He tried to move his arm, but his limbs felt sluggish.

He took out a blade and sliced his wrist. "Don't worry," he whispered. "I'm not going to cut your artery. I don't need to do that. Besides, I want you to stay awake for the show. We can't have you bleeding to death before it's over, can we?"

He cried out as King Dubian squeezed his wrist, draining his blood into an old wound on his finger.

King Dubian cackled. "Now we are truly blood kin." A slight rumble rippled through Coldarius.

"What have you done?"

"I spiked your wine with Oschalot. It's very similar to Ashion, but of course you know that already."

Staring into King Carlomon's eyes, he said, "I've always wondered where Dellah and Opal got such beautiful eyes. Since they didn't come from you, I'm guessing their mother? You'll be meeting her shortly."

He tried to speak, but King Dubian held up his hand. "It's better if you didn't waste what energy you have left on useless words. You're going to die, old king. The Oschalot will kill you in a matter of hours. And then? Coldarius's energy will be absorbed into Platirius."

He tilted his head toward the ceiling. "I wanted you to die slowly so that you could watch your precious Coldarians die from your high tower."

King Carlomon felt his gorge rise. Frantically, he tried to think of a solution but couldn't—the Oschalot was muddling his thoughts. "Dellah showed me a secret passageway before we were married. Since you were so keen on locking me up, you'll have the opportunity to see how it feels."

He paused to look at a couple ChildForms playing in the road. "The best part? No one will find you. But don't worry—you'll be able to see everything. Without the energy that sustains Coldarius—the same energy connected to your life's blood—everyone will freeze to death."

He tried to remove his hand from his iron grasp but couldn't. "I only wanted the merger between Coldarius and Platirius because it's what Dellah wanted. But now, she's gone, and Opal is content to allow me to run things as I please."

He continued squeezing his wrist until the blood pooled on the table before spilling onto the floor. "Now I have them all—Dellah, Opal, and my daughters. I don't need Coldarius anymore. Do you understand? I don't need *you*. Beings praise you as the lifeforce of Coldarius, but to me, you're nothing but dead weight."

"You...are crazy!" spat King Carlomon.

"Mmm. That's what King Anemi told me every day of my lifespan. He said it so frequently, eventually I started believing him. Like him, we'll all be better off without you and your despicable race." He stood up. "Now, let's get you upstairs to watch the show I've prepared for you." He lifted the helpless king onto his strong shoulders and marched him upstairs to the secret passageway.

Grabbing a chair, he set it in front of a one-way window. King Carlomon found that his body refused to move. He stared up at the MaleForm who had married both his daughters, wondering how he allowed him into their lives.

"I don't want you to be saddened by any of this. You'll get to be with your queen when this is all over. It's unfortunate, but you've outlived your usefulness to me. If there's one thing my father taught me, it's that all things come to an end. For you, that time has come. Farewell...father-in-law."

His heart raced when he heard him sealing the door. No one would come for him until the next day. By then, it would be too late...for all of them. For all his lifespan, he tried to be honorable and provide protection for his subjects. But it was all for nothing. He had failed them. He hung his head and wept for what was to come.

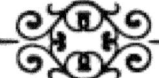

Gallium stood in front of Queen Opal, wishing he hadn't come. He'd tried ignoring her for as long as he could, but soon, she'd begun sending transmissions to his parents. He hadn't liked that. He preferred that Beings dealt directly with him—not his family.

"Gallium, you've finally come to see me," she purred.

There he stood dressed in all black, his heavy pullover and trousers hugging the bulging muscles in his arms and buttocks. His short cropped black hair was pulled away from his handsome face.

Heat pooled between her legs. She moistened her lips in anticipation of—

"You didn't give me much of a choice. Would you mind telling me what you want?"

His surly tone made her pause. *He's still angry about losing Legend. No worries, Darling. I'll make you forget all about her.* "Well, I was wondering if you had a look at the documents my sister drew up for you before she died?"

He was getting bored. Fast. "No, and I assumed they weren't valid once she passed away."

"Oh no, that's not true. Dellah set the stipulations up to last for hundreds of millions of years after her death. No one is allowed to harm you. If they do, they'll die."

"Well, you should make your husband aware of that. He ordered General Kron to kill me years ago and almost succeeded."

"I know. I learned of it shortly after I married him," she lied.

He sighed. "With all due respect, Queen Opal, why am I here?"

She didn't keep him waiting. "I want you to kill King Dubian for me."

He sat down on the expensive cream and platinum divan. None of Queen Dellah's furnishings had been changed. He stared up at the life-sized painting of her hanging above the fireplace.

"You're still harping on that? By The One, you married the MaleForm. You have more wealth and power than any queen in the galaxy. Shouldn't you be happy with what you have?"

"I'll never be happy on his arm. I don't love him, Gallium. You know that. Everyone knows it—even him."

"You knew it, too, before you married him. But love is an illusion. Don't allow it to delude you—it doesn't exist."

She reached over and nudged his thigh. "Oh, come on, you don't really mean that!"

He stared at her.

Flustered, she adjusted the prim collar of her blouse. "I gather Legend's actions hurt you, but—"

"I don't want to talk about her. Not now or ever. This has been interesting, but—" he said, rising from the divan "—if there's nothing else, I'd like to get back home."

She raised her hand. "Wait. I have a surprise for you." She rose and opened the door.

"Gallium!" said Princess Revari, running to him. Princess Vivant followed shortly behind.

"By The One! Look at you, Princess Revari! You've shot up like a flower!" He smiled down at her and tugged on her long braid.

He looked up at Princess Vivant, who was more of a WomanForm than the ChildForm he had remembered. He bowed to her. "Princess Vivant, how have you been? It's been ages since I've seen you."

She flashed a smile reminiscent of Queen Dellah's. "I'm fine, General Barrios. I expected you to look older, but you don't. If one didn't know better, they'd think we were the same age."

"I'm flattered," he said. "But what's with 'General Barrios'? Please call me Gallium, Your Highness."

She lifted an amused eyebrow. "You address me as that, but want me to call you Gallium? I don't think that would be respectful. I don't address General Kron by his first name."

Now what does he have to do with anything? "Well, General Kron wasn't your mother's friend. I was. Please don't feel as if you have to address me so formally."

"That's true. Speaking of friends—all my friends are infatuated with you. They like when you come to Platirius."

His eyebrows raised. "Oh? Again, I'm flattered, but I'm much too old for them. You and your friends are closer to General Kron's age than I am."

Her smile brightened. "Yes, I met him on the night of my father's LifeCelebration. He's very nice."

He kept his smile in check. If General Kron was vying for the princess's affection, that was for King Dubian to deal with. He looked down at Princess Revari. "And how about you? Who do you have a crush on? Whose head do I need to knock together to keep him in line, eh?"

She frowned. "Not me," she declared. "MaleForms are yucky!"

The older Beings laughed.

He rubbed his beard. "Yeah, we can be very yucky, Princess. You stick to your convictions, okay?"

She tugged on his hand. "Okay. Are you staying for supper?"

He looked up at Queen Opal. "No, I'd better get back. I hear your father will be returning soon. I doubt he'd want to see me here."

"He's traveling to Platz," said Queen Opal. "He won't be home for a couple days. Please stay, Gallium. I could put you up in your old bed chamber."

Princess Revari took his hand. "Please, Gallium? The dining staff roasted a whole pig! There's no way I could eat it all by myself!"

Her precocious nature caused another round of laughter.

"Well, since you put it that way, I do love roasted pork. You've twisted my arm."

Princess Revari looked at his arm. "I pity the one who'd try to fight you. Your arm is bigger than both of my legs!"

"It sure is," said Queen Opal. "He's such a big, strong MaleForm."

Ignoring the heat in her tone, he smiled and softly pinched Princess Revari's nose.

"Heyyy," she said.

"What? When you were a baby, you used to grab my nose all the time."

The ChildForm's eyes brightened. "I did?" she asked. He thought she looked just like a miniature version of her mother.

"You sure did," he said.

"Wow, that's amazing," she said happily.

Queen Opal clapped her hands softly. "We'll have supper in the private dining chamber. Princess Revari? Would you like to select the sauces for the pork?"

She grabbed his hand and nodded enthusiastically. "Gallium can sit next to me."

"I'd be honored." He extended his elbow to Princess Vivant. "I'm surrounded by beautiful royal figures. How did I get so lucky? Lead the way, Queen Opal."

As they made their way to the dining chamber, they didn't notice they were being watched. Scowling, General Kron spied Gallium with them. He'd clearly watched him be beheaded years ago. How was it possible he was alive?

He didn't know, but he'd continue to keep watch while King Dubian was away. Once again, Gallium was getting too close to the royal family. Much too close for his liking.

After leaving King Carlomon's palace, King Dubian dispatched a message to King Hitam. In seconds, his face appeared on the TeleScreen. "Why are you calling at this hour? I've surrendered and you've annihilated my army. What more do you want?"

He eyed the bandage covering the wound on his neck left by General Kron. "Yes, you have, but how would you like to live to face another day?"

King Hitam glared at him. "I have no patience for your witless tongue. I heard the queen's death has driven you mad, but if you think you'll absorb Kikhani into Platirius, you'd better think again. My head won't be so easy to take."

"No. I don't believe it will."

"Then why are you bothering me?"

King Dubian's eyes rested on a worried Queen Amori holding their baby daughter. "You still have your family, Hitam. I wish to protect mine. Surely, as a father, you understand the importance of that. We're enemies, but there's another enemy I want to see suffer much more than you."

He cocked his head. "And who would that be?"

His fists clenched. "The one they call Gallium. I want to see him on his knees, begging for his life."

He'd finally succeeded in capturing King Hitam's attention. He had no issue with the Coldarians, but he wanted to see where King Dubian was going.

"I'm dispatching General Iham under a ruse of peace."

"Yes, I'm aware."

"I want you to kill him."

He stared at him. "He is one of your wife's best generals, and much older and more experienced than the ChildForm you sent here to kill me. Why do you want him dead?"

"I want all of the Coldarians dead. Except for Queen Opal, of course."

King Hitam understood. "She has Queen Dellah's face."

"Yes, she does. I want to destroy Coldarius and absorb it into Platirius."

King Hitam and Queen Amori shared a look. "Why in the galaxy would you want to get rid of Queen Dellah's planet?"

"They've caused me a great deal of trouble. I don't intend to let it happen again. I want them all gone. I wish to forget

Coldarius ever existed. It will take time, of course, but the first order of business is to get rid of General Iham. I'll deal with Gallium in my own time."

"If he finds out, he'll kill you. He's the strongest weapon King Carlomon has."

King Dubian's gaze was as vacant and foreboding as Space. "Then I'll just have to ensure that doesn't happen before I destroy all of them."

King Hitam lifted a hand for Queen Amori to sit next to him. "If I help you, what's in it for me?"

"I'll give my approval for you to begin trading openly with other realms again. That includes rebuilding your ranks. When we face each other again, and rest assured we will, I want you to be strong and ready when I finally take your head."

King Hitam glanced quickly at his wife. "All right," he said. "You have a deal. I'll get rid of General Iham, and you'll give me the means to rebuild my army. Out of respect for Queen Dellah, I won't attack Platirius again for a long while. She was a formidable enemy and the greatest commander I've ever faced. She'll be missed."

Queen Amori quietly shed tears for Queen Dellah. They had been friends before their husbands became enemies.

King Dubian stood. "Then it's settled. Send word when it's done." He shut off the TeleScreen and poured another drink. *Soon*, he thought, *Coldarius will be no more.*

A few hours had passed before Queen Amori picked up her baby daughter and went to find her husband. She found him sitting on the bed with his head resting in his hands.

Placing a soft hand on his shoulder, she said, "I saw a Platirian craft outside. Have you and General Iham settled on the terms for the surrender?"

He lifted his head. "Yes. Everything has been finalized. I asked him to wait in the den. I told him I had a burial gift for King Dubian, but it was a lie." Deep sorrow shimmered in his eyes. "I don't want to kill him, Amori. The Coldarians have never harmed me."

"Then don't. Don't do King Dubian's dirty deeds for him. We don't owe him anything, and we can rebuild our army without his help. Whatever war he's waging on the Coldarians, let him handle it on his own."

Shifting Princess Aiki in her arms, she said, "Queen Dellah was my friend. I'd feel terrible if we helped him destroy her planet." She sat down next to him. "We're surrendering, but that doesn't mean we'll never be strong enough to challenge him again."

He reached for her hand and planted a kiss on it.

"Platirius will be yours one day, Hitam. Let's not give up on destroying King Dubian. Please send General Iham home. For me?"

He stood up, pulling her to her feet. "You're the best wife in the galaxy. How did I get so lucky?"

She smiled up at him. "We're the best family around too!" They chuckled as Princess Aiki waved her fist in the air.

"See?" said Queen Amori. "Aiki agrees!"

King Hitam kissed his daughter's mass of unruly curls. "All right. I'll send General Iham on his way. I have a feeling Coldarius will need him for whatever King Dubian has planned. The thought of the Platirians taking another planet sickens me."

"We're making the right decision," said Queen Amori. "Please tell him to give my condolences to King Carlomon."

King Hitam nodded and squeezed her shoulder. "I will."

She peered into her daughter's face and sighed. The Coldarians had always been a peaceful race. She prayed to The One to protect them from King Dubian's antics.

She'd never met Queen Opal, but she suspected she lacked the fire Queen Dellah had. That could prove to be the downfall of Coldarius. As Princess Aiki reached up to play with her earrings, Queen Amori looked up at the stars, hoping she was wrong.

A mos placed another log on the fire. "By the Heavens, is it colder than usual?"

Etienne nodded. "I feel it too. It's strange. Coldarius has always been cold, but it's never been this bad." She patted his arm. "It'll pass."

He hoped she was right. He looked out into the night, unaware that some of the animals were frozen.

She turned on the water and heard a loud crack. She looked up and screamed. The roof, under the weight of heavy ice, collapsed. He pushed her out of the way just before it came down on her. A part of his leg got caught under a large chunk of ice.

"Amos!" she screamed.

Panting, he adjusted his body to ease his leg from under the ice. She reached down, struggling to pull it off.

"Let's lift it together!" she cried. "On one, two, *three*!" They both cried aloud and lifted the ice off his leg. Anxiously, she examined it. "Is it broken? Can you move it?"

Tentatively, he tried to move his leg. A sharp bolt of pain shot up his thigh. "It hurts, but at least I can feel it." He nodded at her. "I can move it around."

She reached for him. "Here, let me help you up." Assisting him to his feet, they looked around at the damage, then up at the massive hole in their roof.

"Have you ever seen such a thing?" she asked. The cold, bitter winds bit at their skin, chilling them to the bone. Startled cries and shouts were mounting around the community. He hobbled with Etienne to open the door.

All around, various homes were caved in by ice and snow. The Coldarians were wandering around outside, bewildered and frightened.

"Is it a storm?" someone shouted.

"If it is, it's unlike anything I've ever seen!" another said.

"We can't stay out here all night! We'll freeze to death!"

Amos looked down at his wife. "We have to make it to the palace. King Carlomon is the energy source for Coldarius. There's enough room there for all of us to keep warm."

She thought of something. "Wait here, I have to take something with us!"

He raised his arm as she darted off. "Etienne! Whatever it is, just leave it! We have to get going!"

She ran to their closet and grabbed the flower Gallium had given her. She promised him not to remove it from its case until she had to. She didn't know why, but she had a feeling they'd need it. She clutched it to her chest, praying that wasn't the case.

His mouth dropped when he saw what she had gone to retrieve. "That's the flower Gallium gave you for JehovRi. That's what you needed?"

She gave him a determined look. "This is no ordinary flower. I don't know how our son knew something would happen, but it may be the key to saving us all." She reached out and grabbed his arm. "Let us go. Lean on me. I see others have started in the direction of the palace already."

Carefully, they journeyed out into the freezing rain and ice. A few slipped and fell and were helped up by their neighbors. More

Beings joined the growing crowd as their homes caved in or fell apart.

When they reached the palace, Etienne nodded at Amos and ran through the gates. She tried to open the palace doors. They wouldn't open.

She turned to the crowd. "The doors are stuck! I can't get inside. Someone please help me!"

A large group of MaleForms tried to beat down the door. "King Carlomon!" one of them shouted. "Please let us in!"

They couldn't get inside the palace. Unbeknownst to them, King Dubian had rigged the doors. He knew as long as King Carlomon was alive, the warmth of the palace would've sustained the Coldarians so their deaths wouldn't be as painful when Coldarius's energy was extinguished.

So did King Carlomon. Through blurred vision, he saw them gathered outside, but they couldn't see him. Tears flowed as he struggled to hold onto his life. If he died, Coldarius would die as well. The Oschalot coursed through his bloodstream, slowing his heartbeat to almost nothing.

He summoned all of his strength to raise one fist in the air—silently willing the Beings he loved to fight for survival. Slowly, his arm lowered to his side and went limp.

The King of Coldarius was dead.

I n an instant, Coldarius went pitch black. Terrified, the Coldarians reached out, trying to find each other in the darkness. Etienne lit a candle.

"By The One! What's happened?" someone cried. A thunderous roar sounded before their world exploded. Hundreds of bodies were hurled into the air before landing on the hard, cold ground.

Amos and Etienne held onto each other as they soared through the air. They landed hard on the palace's steps, with Etienne laying on top of Amos.

"Amos!" she cried. "Amos, are you all right?"

The cries, screams, and moans surrounding her heightened her anxiousness.

"I'm...I'm not okay," said Amos. "I'm...I'm hurt."

She reached inside her blouse, desperately searching for another candle. Then, a bright blue light rose from the ground and floated high above them. It was a blinding, brilliant blue.

The Coldarians found themselves drawn to its calm peacefulness. For a brief moment, they forgot about their physical pain and mental anguish.

Etienne stared at the light, listening to the voices inside of it. They could all hear the soft voices reaching out to them. Reassuring them. Providing comfort. She looked down at the flower, then at Amos. He smiled and nodded. Their long, sweet kiss held all the memories they had made together.

She held the flower in the air as others approached her, mesmerized by its beauty under the soft blue light. Rose Bechelle, holding her InfantForm to her breast, slowly made her way to Etienne.

Soon, everyone who was able to stand surrounded her. She opened the container, exposing the beauty of the flower and its sweet perfume.

With tears rolling down her cheeks, she looked into the faces of everyone she knew and loved. Somehow, they all understood what they must do. Etienne kneeled down and grabbed her husband's hand. Together, they pricked their finger on the thorns and passed the flower to Rose.

Rose pricked her and her baby's finger and passed it to the next neighbor. By the time everyone had touched the flower, most had drifted into a deep sleep. The last one to touch it placed the flower in Etienne's hand and lay down beside her on the soft snow.

They awakened in a magnificent place, filled with tall, beautiful grass and golden roads. Etienne smiled at Amos. "Where are we?"

Amos smiled and squeezed her hand. "We've made it out of the cold." He threw his head back and sniffed the air. "Ah, that smells so fresh!"

Everyone looked around at each other and smiled. They were safe! A Being with bright silver hair came up to them. She was dressed in a long, flowy white dress.

"Hello, everyone! I am Avanance. We welcome all of you. We've waited so long for you to join us."

Etienne looked at the breathtaking bodies of water surrounded by mesmerizing gardens as far as the eye could see. A group of Beings was coming to join them. Everyone looked so happy. She smiled at Avanance. "It's all over now?"

Avanance smiled back at her. "Yes, Etienne. You're all free."

Tears of joy sprang up when she recognized the approaching figures. "Hello, Etienne," they said.

"King Carlomon! Queen Elia and Queen Dellah! You're here with us!"

Queen Dellah laughed and embraced her. "Yes, my friend. We're all here together." She looked around at the smiling Coldarians. "What a glorious time it is!"

Under the caress of the blue light, countless bodies were sprawled out around the palace and throughout the roads. Anyone who hadn't touched the flower had frozen to death in the streets. Some had never made it out of their homes. The blue light continued glowing brilliantly under the darkness of Space.

G eneral Iham saw the light illuminating Coldarius from the craft and tried to get a signal.

"This is General Iham. Does anyone see that blue light? Can anyone hear me? Please respond!" He received no answer. "What in Coldarius is going on?" he muttered.

He sent a signal to Gallium, who was sitting on the floor of the den, playing a game with Princess Revari.

"Gallium! This is General Iham. Do you read me?"

He lifted his palm and received the transmission. "Yes, General. I can hear you. What's going on? Are you still on Kikhani?"

"No! I'm flying over Coldarius. There's a strange blue light that's lighting up everything. Do you know what's going on?"

Gallium and Queen Opal looked at each other. "No, I haven't heard anything about it. I'm on Platirius, but I can leave and find out."

"No! By the time you get over here, I'll know what it is. I'll keep you informed when I find out."

He licked his lips. "Are you sure? If something's wrong, you'll need me."

"I don't know if anything is wrong yet. It could be nothing, but the light is very beautiful. It doesn't look like anyone is in danger. I'll let you know if I need you. I'm bringing back some troops with me from Kikhani. I'll reach out to you within the hour. In a while, Gallium."

"In a while, General Iham." He disconnected the transmission. For reasons he didn't understand, he had an uneasy feeling. A blue light suspended over Coldarius? What could it mean?

Queen Opal was also disturbed by the news. "Princess Revari and Princess Vivant, it's time for bed." She called for the cleaning staff to tidy up the den.

"Aww, do we have to, Aunt Opal? I want to stay and play with Gallium!" said Princess Revari.

She moved closer to the fire to ward off the chill that had come over her. "Gallium will be here in the morning. We can have breakfast in the gardens, but for now, please do as I say and go to bed."

He pinched her cheek. "I'll be here when you wake up, Princess. I promise."

She frowned sadly. Her father never played with her like Gallium. "Okay," she said softly.

"Come, Princess Revari," said Princess Vivant. "We'll go up together."

Princess Revari reached out and took her hand, then quickly leaned down and kissed his cheek. "When I grow up, I'm going to marry you, Gallium," she said shyly.

Amused, he touched his cheek. "I'm honored, but by the time you're all grown up, you'll forget about me. I have a feeling a nice, young MaleForm will steal your heart away."

Her gaze was serious as she stared into his eyes. "I'll never forget you. Not ever."

He stood and bowed to the princesses as they left.

"She's quite smitten with you."

He waved his hand. "Aw, it's puppy love. I give her the attention her father doesn't. I'd be honored to have her as a daughter. It's a shame he doesn't feel that way."

"I still say we should end him. I only married him to secure their futures. I believe you'd make a better king than him any day." She grabbed both of his hands. "They adore you. So do I. A union between us would be much happier for them—and us. We could do it, Gallium. Let's rear my nieces together. You'd be a much better father to Princess Revari than him."

He lowered his head. "I promised Queen Dellah I would take care of her daughters, but I don't know how to be a king. I'm happy with who I am and content with where my life is. One day, one of them will inherit the throne—as it should be. But I'm a Coldarian and I always will be."

She reached up and stroked his beard. "It's Legend, isn't it? You're still in love with her—even though she's gone?"

He looked away. "I'll always love Legend, but she's made her decision. I have to live with that."

She placed his large hand over her heart. "And I love you. I always have. That's why I left for Earth. I couldn't stand being so near you and you always looking through me or around me. I felt I wasn't good enough for you."

But that wasn't true. He decided to play along. There was no point in alerting her about what he knew of her past. If she wanted, she could stop him from seeing the princesses. "How was I supposed to know how you felt when you never told me?"

She glided her soft thumb over the back of his hand. "I was going to tell you how I felt when I returned to Coldarius...but you had already proposed to Legend. I couldn't take it. I returned to Earth to lick my wounds."

He sighed. She rubbed her finger across his bottom lip. "None of us could've predicted what would happen, but we've been given another chance. I know you don't love me and probably never will."

"Queen Opal," he said quietly.

"But we could make it work for the ChildForms, don't you think? I don't have to remain married to him. Just say the word and I won't."

"What a touching scene," said King Dubian coldly.

She stepped back and let go of Gallium's hand. "I didn't realize you had returned from Platz. How long have you been standing there?"

"Long enough to see your pretty face. Gallium, I wish I could say I'm happy to see you, but we both know that would be a lie. It seems stories of your demise were greatly exaggerated. You're excused."

"Don't dismiss him as if he's a servant!" she snapped.

"If he's not a servant, then what is he? He's not royalty." His black gaze penetrated Gallium. "And he never will be. Isn't that right, Gallium?"

He stepped back as a vine whipped from the wall. Taking a life of its own, it began moving swiftly toward him. "What are you doing?" he cried.

Queen Opal's voice entered Gallium's mind. *No, Gallium! He's trying to goad you into killing him. He's already pitted General Kron and the Maieman soldiers against you. He's not powerful enough to kill you, but he can banish you from Platirius. The princesses and I need you! Don't fall for it!*

The sharp point of the plant dropped at the king's feet. Never taking his eyes off him, Gallium said, "I'll be leaving now, Queen Opal. I'll see you in the morning."

He didn't look at a trembling King Dubian as he passed. Struggling to control his rage, he willed himself to concentrate on the princesses. He wasn't sure about Princess Vivant, but he knew Princess Revari needed him.

They were all that was left of his friend. It bothered him that Princess Revari knew next to nothing about her mother. As much as he hated their father, he vowed to remain in their lives. He couldn't let Queen Dellah down. Not again.

"**Y**ou had no right to speak to him that way," hissed Queen Opal. "He makes my nieces happy, why can't you see that?"

"Am I not their father? Do I not go out of my way to ensure they have everything they need?"

"Material gifts—nothing more. You don't spend enough time with them. Throwing your wealth around isn't the same as providing love and support."

He sighed. "I'll try to do better, Opal."

"You always say that but you never do! I don't have time for this. General Iham called in and reported something strange was going on with Coldarius. I'm going to stay awake until I hear from him."

He stilled. "General Iham? He's back from Kikhani?"

She stopped picking up the game pieces to stare at him. "Of course he is. How long did you expect him to stay? His craft should be above Coldarius by now."

Rage flooded through him. *I should've known King Hitam would stab me in the back*! "I'm going to my meeting chamber. I'll get to the bottom of it."

Just as the door opened, a group of cleaning staff entered. "Hello, Queen Opal, we're here to straighten up."

She set the game on a table. "Yes, thank you. I have other things to attend to." She quickly ran off to find Gallium.

King Dubian sat at his desk and pulled up the craft carrying General Iham on the TranScreen. "He's almost to Coldarius," he muttered. "If he reports to Queen Opal, I'm finished! I've come too far to be outsmarted by a commoner!"

He pulled up another screen and zoned in on a tracker under the craft. Smiling, he detonated the bomb. The craft exploded, hurling fast toward the freezing water.

"You won't be reporting anything to anyone, General Iham. Not now or ever." He sat back and grinned. Everything was working out perfectly. In a few hours, Coldarius would be absorbed into Platirius.

He looked up at a life-sized painting of King Anemi. "Do you remember when you told me if I ruled Platirius, it would be similar to that subpar planet, Earth? I wish I could see the look on your face when I earn my BrainStaff. You always thought my brother was better than I. I hope the two of you are burning in hell, watching my triumph."

He poured a drink and lifted it to the painting. "To me! The greatest king to ever sit on the throne of Platirius!" He drained the glass and pressed a button on his desk.

A dining staff answered immediately. "Yes, King Dubian?"

"I smelled roast pork when I arrived. Bring my supper up to my meeting chamber. I want a platter of burnt ends with no sauce, corn, cabbage salad, and potatoes. And add some of Dora Reese's chocolate cake too."

"We'll get it together for you, My King."

"Thank you."

She paused. "You're welcome, Your Highness." She ended the transmission and collected herself. *Wow, he must be in a great mood—he never says thank you!* She hurried to arrange the hot dishes and dessert to be sent to him. She was determined not to get on his bad side. She'd heard the consequences could be fatal.

"Gallium, please wait!" called Queen Opal.

He heard her but couldn't stop walking. On impulse, he decided to report to Coldarius and return to Platirius in time to see Princess Revari. Something was wrong. He could feel it.

He saw the flashes of blue and started running toward it. He reached what should have been the border that separated Coldarius and Platirius, but it was gone!

"What on Coldarius is happening?" he said. Just as he took a step forward, Coldarius lifted up into Space and shattered. A wave of vertigo washed over him as the impact lifted him into the air and flung him to the ground.

"Gallium!" she screamed. The luminous blue light surrounded Coldarius as it exploded again.

She screamed again as the force knocked her to the ground. Large chunks of Coldarius fell away as the planet became engulfed in blue fire. Platirius glowed bright platinum, pulling the fragmented planet closer. The colors merged, creating an electrifying blue haze over Platirius.

Dr. Barrios came running out of the medical chamber toward Gallium. He lifted him off the ground and stared in horror at what was left of their home. Gallium shielded his eyes and looked into the incredible hues.

In the distance, he saw a small hand clutching a flower. Recognition flooded as his heart thudded in his chest.

"Mother!" he screamed, trying to break free of Dr. Barrios's grip. "Motherrrrr!" His wailing rose over Platirius, into Space.

"Mother," sobbed Dr. Barrios. "Gallium, you can't!" he shouted, holding onto him. "You'll never reach it!"

"Motherrrrr! Father!" screamed Gallium.

Dr. Barrios looked around frantically. His eyes found Queen Opal getting to her feet. "Help me! Please help me stop him!"

Her eyes widened. "Father!" she cried. She turned and saw General Kron and the soldiers running from the military chamber. "Get Gallium!" she ordered. "Hold him down! We can't let him fall into Space."

It took the entire army to subdue him. Dr. Barrios released him and ran toward the medical chamber.

"Where are you going?" Queen Opal shouted over the noise.

"No substance will knock him out," he called back. "He'll only listen to one Being!"

Gallium swore, violently flinging the soldiers off him. "Let go of me!" he roared.

General Kron saw the veins beginning to form in his neck and turned to Queen Opal. "If he starts using his powers, he'll kill us all! We'll never stop him!"

"You'd better hold him down or I'll have your neck severed! Do not defy me!"

General Kron cursed. "Try to keep him still!"

"Gallium!" Princess Revari came running out of the palace toward the group of soldiers holding onto him, followed closely by Dr. Barrios.

Queen Opal raised a hand. "Princess Revari!" she shouted. "Don't get in their way, you'll get hurt!"

She reached the soldiers and fell to her knees. "Let go of him!" she ordered.

Immediately, the soldiers let him go and braced themselves.

She reached up and grabbed both sides of his head. "Gallium, look at me!" she commanded. "Look at me, Gallium!"

He stopped shouting and looked down into her face. "My mother," he sobbed. "My mother's up there!"

"It's going to be all right," said Queen Opal. "Please calm down. No one here can defeat you if you use your powers!"

Princess Vivant came running up to them. Tears streamed down Princess Revari's face. She reached out and grabbed her sister's arm. "Gallium has lost his mother like us. Please help him, Vivi. Please?"

Princess Vivant began to cry and kneeled down to Gallium. She laid a hand on top of his head. The power flowed from her hand to his mind. He could feel himself drifting off. He tried to fight it, but the force was too powerful. He succumbed to the calming rays, enveloping him in a deep slumber.

Everyone stared at her.

"What happened? What did you do?" asked Dr. Barrios.

"I placed him into a deep sleep," she said, looking from Gallium to him. "He was in too much mental anguish to handle it all."

Queen Opal nodded to a soldier. "Pick him up and take him to his old chamber in the palace. Don't allow the king to see you transporting him, nor are you to tell him where he is. Have I been heard?"

"Yes, Queen Opal!"

She looked up at the last remnants of Coldarius and covered her mouth. What had happened to their home? She didn't know, but if King Dubian knew what was good for him, he'd better have the answers she wanted to hear.

T he doors flew open to his meeting chamber. He'd just finished his supper and was enjoying watching the absorption of Coldarius. He looked up into her angry face.

"What happened to Coldarius?" she shouted. "Where's my father?"

He steeled himself against her rage. He couldn't allow her to see the slightest bit of nervousness.

"The surveillance team informed me it was an asteroid," he lied. "When it hit Coldarius, it began absorbing its energy. It happened so quickly, I didn't have time to dispatch a rescue team."

She moved closer and looked down at the small feast he had consumed. It looked as if he were celebrating. "General Iham told Gallium he was going to investigate, but he never sent another transmission. What happened to him? And you still haven't told me where my father is!"

He held up his hands. "I haven't heard anything from General Iham in hours, but—at this rate—it's safe to assume that no one survived. I haven't seen King Carlomon in years. I'm so sorry, Opal. I tried to do what I could to save everyone, but I didn't know what was going on until it was too late."

She burst into tears. "Father!" she sobbed.

He moved around the desk and held her in his arms. She sank against him, allowing herself to mourn for everyone lost on Coldarius. Another loud explosion sounded outside the palace.

"That's the last of it," he said softly. "Coldarius is gone."

"It can't be," she wailed. "My home!"

He moved toward the divan and sat with her on his lap. He held her as she wept, not feeling the slightest remorse for what he'd done. King Carlomon and the Coldarians had deserved their fate. Now, Platirius would move forward and would be more formidable than ever.

A NurseForm entered. "King Dubian, I saw the commotion outside. Is there anything we can do for Queen Opal? Would you like us to bring a sedative for her?"

"No," she said. She quickly got off his lap and stood. "I need to see if there are any survivors."

"Darling, please stay here with me. There's nothing we can do right now. Let's wait until morning."

She shook her head. "No, I have to see this through. If there's a chance my father is alive, I have to help him."

He watched helplessly as she turned and left him sitting there. A light began to materialize in the corner. Curious, he moved closer to it. A BrainStaff hovered in the air before slowly traveling to him.

He stretched out his hand and grabbed it. Millions of years of memories filled his mind as the power of Coldarius invigorated him. It was the final step in the absorption process. The kingdom of Coldarius, its Beings—the essence of the planet—was inside of him and Platirius. It was over.

D awn came fast as the last rays of blue hovering over Platirius had almost faded. A soldier met Queen Opal coming across the courtyard. "What did you find out from the surveillance team?"

He was nearly out of breath. "Your Highness, King Dubian lied to us. They never told him an asteroid destroyed Coldarius. It never happened! Coldarius was merged into Platirius. The only way to do this is if another royal figure kills a king."

He panted harshly. "He killed King Carlomon and drained Coldarius's energy. Then he left them all to freeze to death! General Iham's craft exploded over the water. We lost over a million of our Coldarian soldiers!"

I'll kill him! Queen Opal burst through the door. "Is it true? Did you murder my father and everyone on Coldarius?"

He stared at her. "No! I'd never hurt King Carlomon."

Noticing the BrainStaff in his hands, she threw herself at him, clawing at his face. "I knew it!" she roared. "My father died because of you!" He held onto her arms and stood up from the divan. "Take your hands off me. You sick monster!"

"Opal! Who has been putting these lies into your head? I'll have them brought before me and silenced!"

She picked up a glass and threw it at him. "Yes!" she cried. "That's what you do best, isn't it? Silence anyone you please! Too many rumors!" She paced rapidly around the room. "Far too many rumors of you killing your father and brother to take the throne. All these rumors can't be lies, Dubian!"

He calmly stared at her. "Whoever has shared this madness with you will be severely punished!"

"The only madness in my lifespan is what stands before me. What kind of wickedness did I marry into? What are you? Do you even have soul?" She picked up a vase and hurled it at him. Just in time, he ducked.

He tried to grab her again, but she darted away from him. "My Darling. I assure you, this vicious gossip isn't true. I'd cut off my arm before I'd hurt your father—or anyone on Coldarius. It's your home. It's where you and Dellah were born. I am forever indebted to King Carlomon for you. I swear to you, I had no part in it freezing."

Her monstrous stare chilled him to the bone. "If an asteroid caused Coldarius to freeze, then why was it absorbed into Platirius? And why weren't you able to bring everyone here before it did? The BrainStaff you're holding is proof there was never an asteroid!"

"But there was! I didn't know when it was coming or when it landed, Opal," he lied smoothly. "How could I know when I was here? Had King Carlomon told me, I would've dispatched our soldiers and brought everyone here—you know this!"

"What I know is my FatherForm is dead and the surveillance team says they found no evidence of an asteroid landing on Coldarius! He's dead along with everyone I knew back home! The worst part is Platirians are running around saying it was your doing. My own husband!"

"Tell me who told these lies. I will make sure they never hurt you again."

"I'll just bet you will." She snatched away from him. "The only one who has hurt me today is you." Tears of regret filled her eyes. "I never should've married you."

Crestfallen, he grabbed her by the waist. "You don't mean what you're saying! You're getting angry over idle gossip. How could you believe mere commoners over your own husband?"

"Because you kill almost as easily as you lie. What makes you think it's commoners who said it? Do you not know what's said among your own soldiers?"

He stilled at her words. "I don't care who said it. When I find the culprits, I'll have their heads," he said coldly.

She nodded. "If I find you killed my FatherForm, I'll have yours," she promised.

"Opal! Please, listen to me," he pleaded.

She shoved him away. "I mean it. If I find the proof, your head is as good as severed." He watched as she backed away and opened the door. "And then everything you've done will be for nothing. All the power you've absorbed will go to me! I'll make you beg me for mercy. That, King Dubian, is a promise!" She whirled away, slamming the door behind her.

He sighed. It was all falling apart around him. Damn that General Kron! It was his job to keep his soldiers in line. How could he have allowed this to happen? He pushed a button on his desk.

"Yes, King Dubian?"

"Find General Kron immediately and tell him to get his behind to my meeting chamber. Now!"

"Right away, Your Highness!"

Now Opal hated him.

What should I do?

He had to quell the uprising before it started. He'd come too far to lose her. She was the last piece of Dellah he had left. He picked up a glass and shattered it against the wall. No one would turn his wife against him. No one.

General Kron was sitting at his desk when Queen Opal burst into his office with a half-dozen soldiers.

"I'm going to give you one second to tell me the truth or my niece will watch your carcass shipped off this planet in chains."

He blinked. "Your Highness?" Abruptly, he stood, looking at the soldiers behind her. "What is this about, Queen Opal?"

"You're going to tell me exactly why Coldarius was absorbed into Platirius. Don't leave anything out, General, or you'll die before my husband!"

He sank into his chair. "Send them out and I'll tell you everything I know."

In less than an hour, he revealed King Dubian's plan to her. His heart ached as she wept before him.

"I wanted to tell you so many times. But I couldn't betray him. He would've had my title stripped for treason." He rubbed his hand over his head in frustration. "And he would've had me killed."

She dried her eyes and raised her head. "The only one who will die is him. Tonight." She stood over him. "And you're going to help me do it."

King Dubian awakened to the smell of oil burning. Thick smoke surrounded his bed chamber. Coughing, he threw back the bed covers and got on his knees. The bed chamber was on fire! He had to get out! Pacing himself, he dragged himself across the floor to the wall.

Reaching up, he pulled on a secret lever and pushed himself out into the hallway. Someone had tried to kill him! He stood up and ran to the alarm. He pushed the button in rapid succession—signaling for General Kron and the soldiers to report to him.

G eneral Kron sat on the high watchtower with several dozen soldiers. None of them moved when they heard the signal. The Coldarian soldiers were running amok, trashing everything in sight in protest of the fate of Coldarius.

"Aren't we going to stop them?" asked Corporal Leighten.

"No," said General Kron. "Queen Opal gave the order for King Dubian to be executed. We're going to sit back and watch it happen."

Corporal Leighten sat down and showed an impressive sum of funds on his palm. Grinning happily, he looked at his teammates and said, "Okay, let me in this game. If King Dubian dies, we're all going to be very rich MaleForms." The soldiers laughed while General Kron never took his solemn eyes off the palace.

Q ueen Opal retrieved King Carlomon's Azgoate from her nightstand. As the last surviving member of Coldarius's royal family, she wanted to personally kill King Dubian. She whirled around and gasped.

"Dr. Barrios? What are you doing in my bed chamber?"

He had a strange, faraway look in his eyes.

"Did you not hear me?" she snapped impatiently. "I asked what are you doing here?"

He took a step closer to her. "It's your fault. Had you never returned and brought us all here, we could've saved our parents and the others. Now they're all gone and Gallium is losing his mind. I curse you and Queen Dellah for getting us involved with the Platirians!"

He raised his arm to reveal a blade glinting under the lights. She backed away from him.

"I lost my father in the freeze! I've lost just as much as you did, if not more!"

He crept slowly toward her. "No, you didn't. You sacrificed my family so you could have it all. You're mistaken if you think you're going to take advantage of my brother and have him kill King Dubian for you. I won't let you destroy what's left of my family."

He swung the blade, slashing her throat from ear to ear. She dropped the Azgoate, desperately holding her hands to her throat. Blood squirted and pooled down the front of her blouse when she fell to the floor, gasping for air. He waited until she stopped breathing before turning to buzz himself into Princess Vivant's bed chamber.

She had fallen asleep on her stomach, one hand outstretched toward the floor. He gently placed the bloody blade in her hand and backed away. The wing was eerily silent. He paused to make sure no one was coming down the hall before he left.

As meticulous as he was, he never realized someone had seen everything he'd done. They stood looking down at Queen Opal's body for a few moments before quietly exiting the bed chamber.

K ing Dubian rushed into Queen Opal's bed chamber. "Opal, we have to get out of here! They're trying to kill—" He stopped mid-sentence. "No! Oh no, my Love! What's happened?!"

He rushed to her body and turned her over. Expelling an enraged roar, he tried to think of something—anything that would provide a solution. His head snapped up. "My daughters!"

He ran into Princess Vivant's bed chamber and saw the blade in her hand. Shaking his head in disbelief, he removed the blade from her hand. Panting heavily, he rushed into her bath chamber and wet a towel.

After cleaning the blood from her hand, he looked at the trembling blade. Where had it come from? Princess Vivant wasn't violent—she wouldn't have killed her aunt. Someone had tried to frame her. But who?

"Uh, King Dubian, are you in here?" called a soldier.

He went still and crept along the wall. Without making a sound, he craned his neck to peer into the other bed chamber.

Corporal Canob cautiously entered, hoping to find King Dubian and get the bonus Queen Opal had promised for himself.

"By The One!" he said, moving toward the body. "Somebody killed the queen!"

King Dubian knocked him over the head with a heavy statue. He fell to the floor with a thud. King Dubian leaned down and placed the blade in his hand, then retrieved the Azgoate before returning to Princess Vivant's bed chamber.

He lifted her from the bed and carried her down the secret corridor to Princess Revari's bed chamber. Then, lying her next to her sister, he sealed the doors. Sliding down against the bedpost, he waited quietly on the floor. By morning, the queen's body would be found, and the uprising would be quelled.

G eneral Kron found the bodies just before dawn. "By The One, help us all," he said. He looked down at Corporal Canob and shook his head.

"You dumb beast. You just gave King Dubian back his power."

He swore. Once again, the king had escaped his fate. King Dubian ordered Corporal Canob to be thrown into the Flames of Justice and had Queen Opal quietly buried next to Queen Dellah. Without her, the Coldarian soldiers refused to remain on Platirius.

"Come with us, General Barrios," said Sergeant Lionus. "We'll never swear allegiance to King Dubian. He deserves to die for what he did to Coldarius, but now that Queen Opal is gone, there's no one to hold him accountable. General Kron will go to his grave kissing up to him!"

Gallium bowed his head. "Maybe you're right. There's nothing left for me here."

Dr. Barrios touched his shoulder. "The news of Coldarius has circled around. Many kingdoms are willing to take us in. I'll follow you wherever you go."

"Gallium!" It was Princess Revari. She rushed down the palace's stairs and threw herself into his arms. "Please don't go," she begged. "Please don't leave me here."

He looked down into her frightened silver eyes. Queen Dellah's voice came flooding back to him.

Promise me you'll stay by Princess Revari's side for the rest of her lifespan. Never leave her, Gallium. Promise me!

He laid his hand on the top of her head and sighed. When she reached for him, he picked her up and held her. Turning to the soldiers, he said, "You go on. I'm staying here. I can't break my promise to Queen Dellah. The princesses are all that's left of her. They're the last of King Carlomon's bloodline too."

Sergeant Lionus nodded. "I understand, General." He looked at the soldiers behind him. "But we have to go. If we stay, we'll kill him with our bare hands. He can't kill you, but the rest of us don't have special abilities." He saluted Gallium and bowed to Princess Revari. "Let us go!" he said to the troops.

Gallium turned to Dr. Barrios. "Aren't you going to go with them? You don't have to stay here because I've chosen to."

"You're the last of my family. Mother would never forgive me if I left you here with these cretinous Platirians. I'm staying too."

Princess Revari held tightly to his neck. He hugged her before setting her on his feet. "Go on up to your bed chamber and get some rest. I'm not going anywhere, I promise." She gave him a little smile before running up the palace stairs.

"What will we do now, Barrios? How will we go on without them?"

Dr. Barrios pointed. "Look, there's Legend getting off a craft!"

She ran up to them. "Is it really true? Is everyone gone? My mother?"

"Yes, it's true," said Gallium. "Coldarius was destroyed. King Dubian did it, but there's no way to prove it now. He had the all the surveillance staff killed, and someone murdered Queen Opal. There's no one left to make him pay."

"By The One," she sobbed. "Are you two are staying here?"

"Yes, I'm not leaving the princesses."

"Then I'm staying too," she said.

"You don't have to, Legend," said Gallium. "You're free to go wherever you want."

"Where would I go without you?"

His eyes hardened. "It wasn't difficult when you made the decision last time. Don't come back expecting anything from me. I have nothing left for you."

Her eyes glistened with tears watching him storm away from her.

"Give him some time," said Dr. Barrios. "Losing our family has hardened his heart."

"There's no room in it for me anymore—only the princesses," she said sadly.

"You don't know that. None of us know what the future will hold. All we can do is try to survive...together."

Legend watched him walk away with a heavy heart. Coldarius was gone. Nothing would ever be the same.

Epilogue

M any years later, she stood on a hill looking down at
the medical chamber. Dr. Barrios approached her with
caution. Her cold silver eyes seemed to look through him.

"What do you have to report?"

He cleared his throat. "The final dose of Ashion was
administered to him in his breakfast this morning. He won't
survive another hour."

Holding his nervous gaze, she said, "Then it's time."

He felt uncomfortable under the intense scrutiny of her stare.
This time, he could clearly see the hatred burning in her eyes.

"Remain here until I give the signal. Have I been heard?"

"Yes, Your Highness."

"Dr. Barrios?"

He nervously adjusted his collar. "Yes, Your Highness?"

Her beautiful silver eyes reminded him of chips of ice. "It
was you who killed Queen Opal. I watched you slice her neck
open. Then you tried to frame Vivant by placing the blade in her
hand."

He felt his knees buckling. Fighting to control the sporadic
pattern of his breathing, he forced himself to remain calm.

"Had she lived, I would've been spared from much of King Dubian's insanity. In a way, you're directly responsible for everything that's happened to me. In covering up your crime, he spared you from punishment all those years ago. But there's no one who'll save you from me. If you ever give me the slightest reason, I won't hesitate to kill you."

He sank to his knees. "I'm forever in your debt, Your Majesty."

She stared at him for a long time before turning to walk down the path toward the medical chamber. Death had finally come knocking for King Dubian. Princess Revari hastened her steps to open the door.

Author Bio

D.L. Hannah was born in Youngstown, Ohio. She is a writer, entrepreneur, and host of the Amerisogyny podcast. She is a Psi Chi and Alpha Kappa Delta member and earned a Bachelor of Arts degree in Clinical-Community Psychology from Walsh University. For over twenty years, she has been a strong advocate for children diagnosed with Autism. She now lives in North Carolina with her family.

Join D.L.'s VIP List

Join my VIP list @www.dlhannah.com

Also by D.L. Hannah

www.ingramcontent.com/pod-product-compliance
Lightning Source LLC
Chambersburg PA
CBHW071908220626
47052CB00002B/261